About the Author

Teresa Ammons Crew is an award-winning playwright and director with thirty years' experience teaching English and drama at the secondary and university level. She holds a Ph.D. from the University of Wales Trinity St. David, UK, where she specialized in creativity, playwriting, and women's studies with a focus on the works of Kate Chopin.

Her other published works include: *The Silver Phoenix* (full length mystery novel), and the competition plays: *Gym Bags and Other Horror Stories, The Light of the World, Bad Company*, and *Murder at Morose Place.*

Dr. Crew lives with her family in upstate South Carolina, USA.

The Year the World Stood Still

Teresa Ammons Crew

—

The Year the World Stood Still

Vanguard Press

VANGUARD PAPERBACK

© Copyright 2024
Teresa Ammons Crew

The right of Teresa Ammons Crew to be identified as author of
this work has been asserted by her in accordance with the
Copyright, Designs and Patents Act 1988.

All Rights Reserved

No reproduction, copy or transmission of this publication
may be made without written permission.
No paragraph of this publication may be reproduced,
copied or transmitted save with the written permission of the
publisher, or in accordance with the provisions
of the Copyright Act 1956 (as amended).

Any person who commits any unauthorised act in relation to
this publication may be liable to criminal
prosecution and civil claims for damages.

A CIP catalogue record for this title is
available from the British Library.

ISBN 978 1 80016 768 1

This is a work of fiction. Names, characters, businesses, places, events
and incidents are either the product of the author's imagination or used in a
fictitious manner. Any resemblance to actual persons, living or dead, or actual
events is purely coincidental.

*Vanguard Press is an imprint of
Pegasus Elliot Mackenzie Publishers Ltd.*
www.pegasuspublishers.com

First Published in 2024

**Vanguard Press
Sheraton House Castle Park
Cambridge England**

Printed & Bound in Great Britain

For Lily, Eli, and Toby. The ancestors will always be with you.

Chapter 1: **Mediocre** (*adjective*), Common or Ordinary

Stinking *middle* school. She knew if Mom could hear her brain screaming the words, she'd be in trouble for trash talking but she didn't care. Mom hated it when she said words like *stinking,* or *crap,* or *puke.* Mom said those words were crass and crude and an intelligent person should have a broader vocabulary. Well, as far as Abbey was concerned, the word *middle* was worse than crass or crude, it was downright profane. And, even with her broad vocabulary, she knew there was no other way to describe where she stood in her life at that particular moment. *The stinking middle.*

Everything about her miserable life was *middle.* Her hair wasn't black or blonde, it was plain old, ordinary, middle-of-the-road frizzy, ugly brown; she was neither ugly nor beautiful, just plain. Her little brother, Levi, was small for his age. If he'd been a girl, he would have been called *petit.* He had beautiful, silky black hair and skin like porcelain. Nothing about her was sleek, silky, or porcelain. The only above average things about her were her height (she was taller than all of the boys in her grade, *so embarrassing*), and her big feet that refused to stop growing.

Still not finished complaining, Abbey contemplated further evidence of the uninteresting dullness of her life. *How about this tidbit: my hometown, Trinity Hold, North Carolina, is smack dab in the (you guessed it), middle of North Carolina. Drive three hours west and you arrive at The Blueridge Parkway in North Carolina's mountains, three hours east and you're at the beaches of the Atlantic Ocean.* Location. Location. Location.

In another month, summer vacation would be over and she'd join the ranks of thousands, heck, probably millions of school kids around the world who'd re-enter the abyss that called itself *middle* school. What education genius thought up such a crappy concept? Way to go whoever you were, nothing makes a kid feel special than telling them up front, "You're not a cute little elementary-school kid anymore, you're not a cool teen-aged high schooler, nope, you're just a nondescript, nothing to see here, *middle* schooler."

And, in Abbey's case, not *just* middle school. This year she'd be in 7th grade. The *middle* of *middle* school. Could life be any crueler? What had she done to be so dumped on (another of her mom's hated crudities), by the universe? For once, couldn't karma give her a break and send some positivity her way?

She slammed her notebook shut after ripping out the three pages of 'I HATE MIDDLE SCHOOL,' she had written on every single line of each of those pages. She wadded the note paper into a ball, threw it at the garbage can in the room she shared with her stupid little brother, missed the shot, then threw the entire notebook on the floor.

"Abbey? Abb-eeeee!" Levi, her seven-year-old pain in the patootie brother finally gave up screeching her name and thumped down to sit against the door of their room. The carpet was old and dusty and she knew he shouldn't be sitting on the floor; it would aggravate his asthma. She used to vacuum it, back before their vacuum broke down; lately she'd had to try to sweep it and that just wasn't cutting it.

She went to the door and jerked it open. Levi, as was expected, fell over into the tiny bedroom. "Get up, pest. You know Mom told you not to sit on the carpet until we get the vacuum fixed."

"It isn't cost effective to have a vacuum repaired these days. Vacuums are like phones now, they're cheaply manufactured. They're not meant to last a lifetime. You're just supposed to throw them away when they break and buy new ones." He shook his asthma inhaler in vain, trying to coax every last drop of the medicine to spray just one more time. Mom was going to get his prescription filled for a new one as soon as she got paid. Three days away.

Levi always talked like he was a television news anchor. He had two copies of the dictionary and he read them every day like they were storybooks. His goal in life was to be the national spelling bee champion. At least he had a goal, even if it was a dumb one. That's more than she had.

She'd had goals. Once upon a time. Like the fairy tales always say. When she was little, she wanted to be a princess. Then a ballerina. Then, when she started pre-K, she wanted to be a teacher like Miss Carvell. She adored Miss Carvell and cried her heart out when she learned that graduating from pre-K meant leaving the familiar safety of Miss Carvell's classroom to go to elementary school. To add insult to injury, Miss Carvell had gotten married, so she wasn't even Miss Carvell anymore.

Why did life have to keep changing? As soon as she got used to something or someone, wham! Everything up and changed on her. She had just gotten acclimated to elementary school when she had to enter stinking middle school. She'd finally managed to make one friend in 6th grade. Her friend, Drew, was funny and nice and not stuck up at all even though her family was sort of rich (big brick house with a pool out back). However, at the end of the year, thank you universe very much, Drew's dad got a new job in another state so, bye, bye bestie.

She and Drew promised to keep in touch but Abbey knew they wouldn't. Abbey didn't have her own cell phone and it would be dumb for Drew to text Abbey's mom. So, when the two girls said their tearful goodbyes, they promised to email but both of them knew they'd probably never speak to each other again. *Email? Give me a break.* Abbey thought email was barely a step above snail mail. Nobody under eighty years old used email.

"Want to know what my new word for today is?" Levi asked. He hated it when Abbey was so grouchy. He knew it was his fault for being annoying but he just couldn't seem to stop doing that. Sometimes, she smiled at him if he only said the right thing. It was very difficult to keep coming up with witty things to say but he refused to give up. He needed Abbey to love him as much as he loved her.

"With all my heart and soul," Abbey said. Levi looked crestfallen at the sarcastic quip. He was so darn touchy.

"Sorry, little dude. I didn't mean to be such a grouch. I really do want to know what your new word for today is."

"Really? It's *panacea*. Do you know what it means? Sorry. You're in middle school, of course you know what it means."

"Humor me," Abbey replied.

"It means something that's a cure for everything! Absolutely everything! Boy, wouldn't it be great if we had a panacea for everything that's rotten in life?"

For the first time ever, Abbey took a long look at Levi. He was only seven years old; how did he know life sucked? She hadn't learned that valuable lesson until she was at least nine. OK, not counting the day their stupid father walked out. Sure not bringing that memory back. She had never considered that Levi was anything other than a little brother, or, as Peppa Pig would say *a little bother*.

She picked up the hairbrush off the dresser, touched Levi on both shoulders, and said, "I knight thee, Sir Panacea. Go forth and make the world a beautiful, happy place."

Levi took the hairbrush and with a flourish said, "Crappy carpet – be gone!"

Abbey said, "Crappy, tiny bedroom – be gone!"

Levi took the brush, ran down the hallway and said, "Crappy broken down television – be gone!"

By the time they finished be-going everything, they sank into the tired old brown Naugahyde sofa, laughing.

Levi whispered, "Wish there was a panacea for whatever's wrong with Dad."

Abbey was angry, Levi had broken their good mood by mentioning he who must never be mentioned again. Dad had been gone for over five years, why did Levi refuse to abandon the hope that Dad would ever come around again? How could he even remember who their dad was? Levi had barely been walking when Dad had fallen in love with 'The One and Only Barkley's World-Famous Carnival,' when it had passed through town. After three days of stink and noise and fun for the whole family, Barkley's tents and rides and food vendors had packed themselves up and left with one extra attraction (their dad), tagging along.

Ladies and gents, step this way to see the incredible missing father. He turns his back! He leaves without warning! He loves traveling with strangers more than he ever managed to love the woman he married and the two children he helped bring to life! Yessiree, he's a grown man untethered to family and pesky responsibility. Footloose and fancy free, as Gran used to say, with nary a backward glance.

The first year after he'd left, Abbey and Levi both received birthday cards from him from Reality, Arkansas with lots of X's and O's for hugs and kisses. The second year, no birthday cards but a holly jolly Merry Christmas! card from Last Stop, Oklahoma, addressed in some kind of fancy handwriting to Mrs. Rose Whit and children, like he'd forgotten what his children's names were. The rest was silence.

"There's no panacea for what's wrong with our dad. He's a no-good, rotten person. He deserted all of us. May as well mark him off your list of things to be hopeful for. For all practical purposes we don't have a dad. The sooner you face that, the better off you'll be. Every time you mention his name it makes Mom cry and makes me so mad I could spit. So, just cut it out, OK?"

Abbey feared Levi would never give up hoping for their dad to be a decent human being, and she felt bad about making him cry, but, hey, life was tough. Get used to it. With Mom working so much, Abbey had to spend more time with Levi than ever and she was determined to do right by him.

Mom would be home in about thirty minutes, so she needed to get started on dinner. Mom was paying her twenty dollars a week to babysit Levi. That included general house cleaning, laundry, making his breakfast and lunch, and starting dinner for the three of them. She was desperate to earn enough money to buy a cell phone, so she was determined not to mess up this gig.

Levi, head hanging low, walked back to their bedroom. He'd find comfort in his precious words, she knew. She started to apologize to him but thought better of it. Apologize for what? For telling the cold, hard truth? She felt miserable and bummed that she'd made him feel the same. Nope, not *her*, it was their miserable dad who'd turned their happiness into tears. And, did he ever feel guilty for deserting them? Not a chance. Not that any of them could even ask him.

She took the three steps from the living room into the tiny kitchen. Living in the world's smallest apartment had its drawbacks (sharing a bedroom and bathroom with her brother), but also its perks (she was able to keep the place spotlessly clean and shiny, except for the dusty carpet – truly not her fault), with very little time or effort.

She preheated the oven to 350^0. Then, she powered up the small screen on the laptop the school loaned them because some grown-ups were freaking out about some new flu-bug that had managed to hop, skip, and jump across the ocean that they'd cancelled in-person classes and made everybody finish the year online. In an effort to try not to make the 'poor,' kids (*like me and Levi*, Abbey thought), feel bad about not having computers at home (*again, like me and Levi*), the school had loaned everybody a laptop to keep at home so they could actually get online in order to do online school.

Whatever. They weren't fooling anybody. The rich kids knew they were rich and the "poor kids," knew they were poor. Duh. Abbey was just glad to have a laptop at home. She went to the website she'd pinned to her task bar and searched the quick and easy dinners tab she'd saved to her favorites. The first few weeks of summer vacation she'd made frozen pizzas and French fries about every night but then, one day, she discovered the *Savor the Flavor: Modern Meals for Modern Families* website and a light bulb went off inside her brain.

Every Saturday, she now made menus for the upcoming week's meals. Then, she and Levi and Mom went grocery shopping together. *How pathetic*, she thought. Food shopping was the highlight of her week, she actually looked forward to it. She loved the planning as much as the shopping and preparation. Levi refused to eat any food that had once had a mother, so she was leaning pretty heavily on vegetarian meals which, she had to admit, she actually enjoyed. Figuring out the puzzle of what was on sale each week, how to be creative and diverse with her food choices, and creating meals that all three of them would eat was kind of fun. In a sad, man I need to get a life, way.

Tonight, she was making steamed broccoli and cauliflower over cheesy rice. She took rolls out of the freezer and buttered them, then washed the vegetables and put them in the good frying pan with a little olive oil. She had two frying pans but one of them made everything stick so she tried her best to make one-pan meals. Her mom had gotten a rice cooker for a wedding present a hundred years ago but had never even taken it out of the box until Abbey took over cooking. It had proven indispensable to Abbey's growing culinary achievements.

"Hey, squirt," she called out to Levi. "What's a seven-letter word for food?"

"Cuisine," he answered without a second's pause. "Give it up, you'll never stump me!"

You are so full of yourself, she thought. And, without realizing she was doing it, she smiled.

Chapter 2: *Matriarchy (noun),* Female Head of Family or Group

Mom came in, threw her bag on the coffee table, walked into the kitchen and kissed the top of Abbey's head. "Mmmmmm, smells delicious! You're really turning into a master chef, Abbey. I'm proud of you. You remind me of my mom. She was a great cook. Maybe you got it from her. Must skip a generation, Lord knows I didn't get any cooking genes." Then, almost as an afterthought, she added, "Sure wish you remembered her."

"I remember her. A little," Abbey said.

"I wish she was still with us. I miss her as much now as I did when she left us seven years ago. And she loved you so very much, Abbey," Mom talked about death like it was a trip to the beach. Abbey thought maybe her mom was superstitious or something. Maybe that was why she never said the word *died*. Abbey was more realistic than her mom. She knew Gran hadn't left them, she'd died. Plain and simple.

"I wish she was still alive. Then, she could babysit Levi and I could go get a real job somewhere," Abbey said. Mentioning getting a job always made Mom angry so Abbey wasn't surprised that mom went on defense.

"You're only twelve years old, Abbey. You can't get a work permit until you're at least fifteen. And I don't want you doing 'a real job,' anywhere. I want you safe, at home. Being home with your family is more important than making money." *How in the world did I raise a kid who was so obsessed with money? Where did I go wrong?* she thought to herself.

Rose was often exasperated with her daughter and at a complete loss as to how to communicate with her, how to relate to her in any meaningful way. Which, in turn, made her feel guilty and question every decision she made. Levi was certainly an easier child to deal with but his natural tendency for solitude worried her. Sometimes she felt inadequate as a mother, overwhelmed by the burden of responsibility which rested solely on her shoulders. If only she had her own mother's nurturing wisdom. If only her own mother hadn't been snatched away from her suddenly and horribly and much too soon. Cancer was pure evil. She hated it with all her being and begged God to spare her children from whatever DNA flowing through their veins might contain that vicious disease.

Knowing both her parents were in heaven was a given, she had never worried about their final fate. However, she needed the comfort of their presence, their wisdom, as much now as she ever had. Sometimes it was difficult not to question why God had taken them when she needed them so desperately.

Blind faith often proved to be elusive for Rose.

She worried that when the time came for her children to grow up and move away, she would be completely rudderless and unmoored. She feared Abbey and Levi would follow her husband's example and abandon her for greener pastures. She had no idea where Sam was, since he hadn't deigned to contact her (except for that humiliating time he showed up at her work demanding to speak with her manager), after he signed the divorce papers, so she honestly didn't know what color his pastures were. Nor did she care. He had signed away all of his parental rights without even a pretense of protest. In her mind, that made him a monster and she would never understand nor forgive him.

She sent up a silent, heartfelt prayer for God to protect her children and make her become a better mother. To give her child rearing advice. To give Levi a good dose of self-assurance, he really was an extraordinarily intelligent child, he just didn't seem to know it. And to make Abbey, what? Less touchy? A little more patient or loving? Less gloom and doom? When it came to Abbey, Rose didn't even know what to ask for. So, she just prayed, *Dear God, you gave her so much talent and ability. She doesn't seem to understand the strength of her personality. Please help her see the path You want her to go down. Please help Abbey be happy.*

"Money isn't the most important thing in the world, Abbey. It isn't even in the top ten," she said.

"Yeah, right. Making money's not important to anybody on the planet, is it?" Even thinking about money made Abbey's head hurt. "Truce?" she asked. She knew how impractical her mom was, she'd never listen to reason. Another gift from the universe: Abbey, the kid, was the reasonable, realistic one while her mom, the adult, was so naive about the ways of the world. Mom just had that blind faith that money didn't matter, God was in His heaven, and all was right with the world.

"Truce," Mom replied. "Anything going on around here I need to know about?"

"Prince Charming dropped by again with that ridiculous shoe and I had to threaten to call the police if he didn't stop stalking me. The bank called and said they'd made a mistake in our account and we needed to add another million bucks to our savings. Same old, same old."

Levi heard their voices and came bounding into the kitchen. He always greeted his mom like she'd been gone for a year. He was just so darn *happy* to see her. Weirdo.

He skidded to a stop just in time to keep from knocking his mom off her feet. He hugged her with all his might.

Mom wrapped her arms around Levi. "Oh, my goodness. I sure missed you today."

Levi cast his eyes upward, as if staring up at a long-lost friend. "What's a nine-letter word for the female head of the family?" He jumped up and down in excitement, hoping to finally stump Mom.

"Matriarch," Mom answered.

"That puts you at about ten thousand to zero," Abbey said to her brother.

Levi didn't rise to the bait. He apparently didn't care if Mom stumped *him*. Abbey would never understand his blind devotion. Once again, the notion she was the only logical one in the family was reinforced. Blind devotion to anything or anyone only got you hurt. Because people you give your heart to always up and leave you. She had learned that the hard way. And, boy oh boy, she'd never make that mistake again.

Too much mushy stuff going on around here, she thought. "Levi's asthma inhaler is empty," she said out loud. She thought that'd bring the two dreamers back to reality.

Mom got down on her knees to look Levi in the eyes. "Oh, honey. Why didn't you tell me? Remember, you promised you'd watch the counter on the side of the cylinder? Remember, it counts down each time you use it and lets you know how many doses are left? You promised to let me know when you got down to five. We can't let that medicine run out, Levi. It's very important. You're a big boy now, you can handle that responsibility, can't you?"

"I'm sorry, Mom. I thought I could make it until you got paid. I know we can't afford it right now," Levi said.

Mom looked like she was choking on something. Her face and neck got all red.

"Maybe he'd act more responsible if you'd quit treating him like he was a baby. He's seven-years old, Mom. For Pete's sake. And anyway, you're the mother, maybe you should be the one to keep up with…"

Mom cut her off before Abbey could finish her sentence. "Abbey, enough!" She got up off her knees and turned to look squarely at Abbey. "Enough of your mouth, young lady. You aren't the adult here. You are so disrespectful. I'm tired of it."

If you want to receive respect, you have to give it first. Abbey dared not say the words out loud, there was twenty dollars on the line here. She turned her back on the love birds and put serving spoons in the rice and the vegetables. Usually, she put their food out in pretty bowls and brought it to the table. Tonight, she just didn't give a flip. Let both of them dish their food out straight from the stove. She was the one who did all the work around here and nobody appreciated it. *Maybe that's why dad left,* she thought. *Tough to stick around when nobody appreciates you. Maybe I need to take a hike too. Then Mom would see how much I do for her.*

Tears were rolling down Levi's cheeks. He was so tender-hearted. He couldn't handle confrontation.

Smoke was escaping from the door of the oven. *Great. The rolls are burned. I hope you're happy.* Abbey's good mood was ruined now. She turned off the stove and took the rolls out of the oven, slamming the bread pan down on the tiny kitchen counter. "Enjoy your meal."

She flounced out of the kitchen, down the hall, into her bedroom. The stupid door was warped a little so she wasn't even given the satisfaction of being able to slam it shut.

"Abbey, please come and eat with us. As a family. You know how important that is to me." Mom always threw the family card on the table every time Abbey tried to make a point about the dysfunction going on around here. Mom didn't want to hear it.

"Not hungry," Abbey called back from her room, nope, correct that, from *their* room. Jeez, twelve years old, going on thirteen, and she still had to share a room with her brother. What a disaster her life was. She couldn't wait until she was old enough to get out, get a place of her own. That'd show 'em.

The lamp on her nightstand winked on and off. Been doing that a lot lately. *Stupid, cheap piece of junk.* She pointed at the lamp and said, "Crappy lamp, be gone!"

Do you feel better now? Did that little tantrum of yours accomplish what you'd hoped for?

Great. Now the constant irritant speaks. For several weeks Abbey had been hearing this annoying voice in her head. She had dubbed it her constant irritant after Levi had stumped her with the word *irritant*, she decided it was the perfect word for that stupid voice. Sometimes she thought maybe she was going crazy or something. Hearing voices like some kind of psycho. In desperation, she'd googled "hearing voices in your head." And found that lots of people heard voices. Some psychiatrists called this phenomenon "the inner voice." Supposedly, it was natural for most everybody. Just a part of what it takes to make you a human being.

She'd also read that some doctors believe your inner voice is just the id and ego battling it out for control of your actions. She hadn't bothered to try to find out what id and ego actually meant. It was too complicated. Preacher Johnson called the voices *good* angels and *bad* angels. He theorized that everybody struggled every day to stick with the good angel because the devil was always whispering in our ears to make us think, say, and do bad, mean stuff.

Normal or not, id or ego, angel or devil, Abbey hated it when that voice spoke up. Always putting her down. Sometimes it didn't seem to be coming from inside her own head, it often sounded like somebody was outside her head looking in. And making annoying comments.

Shut up! You are so irritating! She covered her head with pillows to try to drown out the voice.

Mom knocked on the bedroom door. "May I come in?"

"Yes, ma'am. It's your house. And the door isn't even closed," Abbey answered.

"When you get over feeling sorry for yourself, please come and eat. Levi said you didn't eat lunch today, so I know you're hungry. And, after supper…"

Before she could finish that sentence, Abbey interrupted her, "I didn't eat lunch because I had too much housework to get done before you got home. Happens a lot."

"Abbey," Mom began, "Let's not fight." Things will get better. I promise."

"How can you promise that, Mom? Exactly what in the universe do you have control over? You shouldn't make promises you can't keep." As soon as she said it, Abbey knew she'd gone too far and was angry with herself for deliberately hurting her mom's feelings.

"I can promise you that you're the most special girl in the world and I will always love you. I can also promise you that after supper I'm going to the drug store to get Levi's inhaler refilled then stop by Hannigan's on the way home for ice cream. Levi and I are going, with or without you."

Abbey's stomach growled loudly so it would have been dumb to keep saying she wasn't hungry. She got up off her bed, went to the bathroom and washed her face. With as much dignity as she could muster, she joined her mom and brother in the kitchen and ate supper. No need to be a martyr. Hannigan's made the best banana split in the world; she'd be stupid to miss out on that.

The constant irritant whispered, *see, that wasn't so difficult, was it? No need to cut off your nose to spite your face.*

Don't know what that means, Abbey thought back to that aggravating voice. *So go away and stay away.*

Not going to happen, the irritant replied. *You need me now more than you ever have. I'm not going anywhere. Things around here are about to change and get real scary real fast and you're going to need all the help you can get.*

You're an idiot, Abbey thought back at the darn voice. *Nothing ever changes around here. And, I've never needed anybody's help for anything.*

Chapter 3: *Permutation (noun)*, The Process of Change

The next afternoon, Mom came home from work early. Abbey couldn't remember that happening, ever. Rain or shine, sick or well, Mom went to work every day and stayed until quitting time. She believed fudging on the time actually spent doing what you were getting paid to do was cheating and lying. And, Rose Whit wasn't a cheater or a liar. A feeling of dread ran down Abbey's spine. *Please don't let Mom lose her job,* Abbey thought.

"Family meeting!" Mom called out to Levi and Abbey.

They joined Mom around the kitchen table.

"As you know," she began, "when my mother, your Grandma Emma, or rather Gran, passed on, she left her house to me, to us, but we didn't move into it. Your, well to be truthful, your father didn't want to live in Gran's house. He, um, he thought we'd be happier staying here, in town, in this apartment. He felt the house was old fashioned and needed too much work to make it functional."

"I was just barely born," Levi said.

"She knows that," Abbey snapped. "Get on with it, Mom. What's going on? Did Gran's house burn down or something?"

"No, the house didn't burn down. You are such a pessimist sometimes, Abbey," Mom went on to explain about how Dad had wanted to sell the house but she had refused to sell so they finally reached a compromise. They rented the house out. Long-term lease.

"This morning," Mom continued, "a lawyer called and told me the tenants wanted out of the lease. The wife got a job opportunity on the west coast and they want to know how much I'd charge them to break the lease before the ten-year term is up. So, what do you think?"

"What do we think about what?" Abbey asked. "You've been raking in rental income every month for seven years and we've been scrimping and saving and living in this dump and we can't even afford a cell phone for me? I think that sucks. That's what I think."

"I haven't been 'raking in money', Abbey. I've put half the rental income into college savings for you and Levi. With the rest, I've paid insurance and taxes, upkeep on the property. I've taken as little as possible to augment my income for necessities like the rent on this place, food and school supplies and Christmas – you have no idea how much money it takes to keep a family going."

"So, the thing is, we, the three of us, need to make a decision about what we want to do with Gran's house. We can rent it out again, put it up for sale, or, we could move into it and live there. It's a big decision and I think we should make it together. But, before we do, I'm going to take you both over and let you look at it. Levi, you haven't been there since when you were a tiny baby and I don't know how much you remember, Abbey."

"I remember going to Gran's house. I don't remember exactly how to get there. Doesn't matter though. I say, take the money and run," Abbey said. "Sell the sucker and use the money to move out of this place. And buy me and Levi decent phones and computers. I'm sick of living in an old, run-down dump. Let's go high-tech and modern for a change. Stone and steel and lots of sharp angles and glass. No curtains. I really like that look. It's super-cool."

Mom rolled her eyes. "Life is more than money and 'stuff.' And new and modern doesn't necessarily mean new and improved. We aren't making a decision until *after* we visit the house. Levi, go brush your hair and put on shoes. Abbey, get your purse and lock up behind Levi. I'll meet you both at the car. Bring your masks."

Freaking stupid masks. Another thing Abbey would be thrilled to leave behind when this nightmare epidemic or pandemic, *whatever*, ended. Abbey tried to reason out this conundrum: surgeons always wear masks when they operate, so there must be some sound reasoning, some scientific principle to explain why wearing a mask helps keep a sterile environment sterile. Germs travel through the air, but air still flows through masks or the surgeons would all suffocate and die before they could finish up with their surgery. So, how can a strip of paper over your mouth and nose keep deadly germs away from you?

Maybe if she was a child prodigy like Levi, she could have figured it out but for her feeble, non-brilliant brain it didn't make sense.

I'll go look but I can tell you right now I want to sell the old place. It's probably falling down by now anyway. Sell it, use the money to move out of here. Nothing you can do or say can make me change my mind about that, Abbey thought. She waited for her constant irritant to scold her but it remained silent. *Knew it'd be a waste of time*, Abbey told herself.

Gran's old house was about eleven miles away from their apartment. Abbey remembered going to visit her grandma when she was little. The trip had been excruciating. It seemed to take an eternity. She always fell asleep on the way to Gran's.

This time the trip didn't take any time at all. As soon as they pulled up in the driveway Abbey's mind flooded with images of her grandma rushing out to greet her with a hug and kisses. She remembered how good Gran's house always smelled. Like chocolate chip cookies and fresh flowers and something else Abbey couldn't quite articulate. *Love*, her constant irritant whispered. *This house was filled with love.*

Gran's house was a two-story craftsman-style that had been built by Abbey and Levi's great-great-grandfather, Raymond. He was a master craftsman and the care and attention he put into the home was readily apparent. There was a large front porch with a swing, shutters that were held open by what Mom called shutter dogs, beautiful, mullioned windows of leaded glass, and a huge transom over the front door. Mom said there were transoms over all the doors downstairs to aid in air flow because when the house had been built there was no air conditioning. And, of such importance to their mom, their grandmother had been born here, in this very house.

Abbey walked up to the front porch and her heart lurched inside her chest. The porch lights, which were still on from the night before, winked off. She turned to look at her mother, and heard herself blurt out, "We need to live here, don't we? This is where our home was all along." *Where had that random thought come from?*

Mom just smiled.

Levi bounded up the steps to the porch and jiggled the doorknob. He let go when the door opened and a tall, thin man dressed in a business suit stepped out to greet them. "Oh, hello. You must be the Whit family. Our solicitor said you may pop over today."

He spoke with some kind of accent that Abbey couldn't place. She'd never met anybody from anywhere other than North Carolina so she couldn't be sure where this guy came from. England, maybe.

Mom shook the man's hand and said, "Good to meet you, Mr. Longstreet. I'm Rose Whit and these are my children, Abbey and Levi."

Mr. Longstreet ushered them into the house. While he and Mom talked, he invited Abbey and Levi to go exploring. Abbey could feel her heart vibrating inside her chest. She wanted to come back here, to live here, so badly she could hardly contain herself. *What is it about this place?* She didn't know and she didn't care. She only knew she wanted to be here.

By the time their mom and Mr. Longstreet finished their conversation, Abbey and Levi had picked out their bedrooms. What a luxury! There were three bedrooms in the house. They could each get their own room! The kids would still have to share a bathroom but neither cared. They'd have their own room and a *yard.* Levi was most excited about the yard. Abbey, of course, was most excited about having an entire bedroom, a kingdom of her own, to rule over as she pleased. She started making plans on how she could hide out in her room any time she wanted to.

"Please tell me we can live here, please, please, please!" Levi begged.

"It's a big decision," Mom reminded him. "You'd both have to change schools. Are you OK with that?"

To which he replied, "Yes!"

Abbey shrugged and said, "A school by any other name would stink as bad. No big deal."

Mrs. Longstreet, a high school English teacher who had joined them in the foyer, laughed out loud. "A young Shakespeare fan! A rarity these days."

"Abbey is indeed a rarity. In any days," Mom replied.

Abbey, who thought she wasn't even capable of doing it, blushed. "We had to read *Romeo and Juliet* in school last year. Nothing rare about it. Jeez, calm down, will ya."

And so, the die was cast. None of them knew that, in addition to the school situation, their entire lives were about to change. For better or for worse, the rest of their lives would be measured as *before* and *after* they moved into Gran's house.

Mr. and Mrs. Longstreet (who were, by the way, from Australia), went on and on about how much they had loved living in Gran's house and hated to leave it. They told Abbey and Levi how lucky they were to be moving into such a great home.

Abbey couldn't resist the urge to downplay her excitement, "I wouldn't say 'lucky'. It's more like, kinda' cool to get a change of scenery. Nothing lucky about moving. Different place, same old life."

You just have to be contrary, don't you? the constant irritant scolded.

"Shut up!" Abbey hadn't meant to say that out loud. She just wanted that darn voice to get out of her head and shut the heck up.

Mr. and Mrs. Longstreet, her mom and Levi, all looked at her like she was crazy.

Mom hastily apologized for Abbey's rudeness, took her hand like she was a little kid and pulled her down the sidewalk to the car. "What on earth is wrong with you, Abbey? Why did you tell the Longstreets to shut up? I'm so embarrassed and you are so grounded."

"I didn't tell them to shut up. I swear on a stack of Bibles. I was talking to myself. Never mind, you wouldn't understand. You never believe me. I'll never be the good kid. Levi's your dearly beloved perfect one. And, grounded? Swift move, Mom. Unless you cancel that dream trip you had planned to take us all to Disney World, grounding is meaningless. Like, where, exactly, do I go? And seeing as how I'm practically the poorest kid in school, I don't have a phone for you to take away. I'm already a prisoner in the suckiest life imaginable."

"You just got another day added to your grounding, poor, poor prisoner Abbey. Now, get in the car." Rose wondered if corporal punishment would possibly work on a twelve-year-old with delusions of adulthood. *She's so darn stubborn, it'd only make her more firmly entrenched in what she deems justifiable self-pity. Besides, if anybody saw me actually spank her they'd call Child Protective Services and my worst nightmare scenario, being separated from my children, would become a reality. My kids in foster care. Sam Whit would have a field day with that. And my mama would roll over in her grave.*

She looked in her rearview mirror as she backed out of the driveway. Abbey had scooted as far away from Levi as possible and was scrunched up against the car door as if she was trying to meld with it. *Maybe a stint in foster care would fix Abbey's attitude problem. Nah, not a chance. God help me, my precious baby girl is turning into a rebellious stranger. Please, please tell me how to pull her back from this disastrous path before she goes so far away, I'll never be able to reach her. Hang in there, Abbey. Your mama loves you and I know you're having growing pains and I know they're real and they are excruciating but, this too shall pass. I hope.*

Abbey's face bore the countenance of a maelstrom of anger that had mixed with an emotional thunderstorm. Her temper was like quicksilver. Rose wondered if maybe this was the cup of trembling and she and Abbey both would have to drink from it before their family would be made whole again.

Chapter 4: *Trepidation (noun),* Anxiety or Alarm

Abbey sulked in her room for two days. She only came out to go to the bathroom and cook meals for her brother and her jailer. She was so close to having money for a phone, she wasn't going to ruin that now. She refused to sit at the table and eat with the enemy. Instead, she snuck out of her room at night and raided the fridge. No retreat. No surrender. That was her new motto.

On the fourth day, her grounding ended but she remained stubbornly entrenched in her self-imposed isolation. Mom came home from work early again, not a good sign. Mom's job at the bank was a crummy one, just answering the phone and doing paperwork for a tiny bit more than minimum wage but a crummy salary was better than no salary at all and Abbey felt fear rise up in her belly.

She met her mom at the front door. "What's wrong? Why are you home early? Did you lose your job?" Abbey had been keeping up with the media reports about this weird flu-thingy that'd scared the daylights out of people all around the world. News junkie, she was not. Too boring. But sometimes helpful. There were reports about people everywhere losing their jobs because of that virus whatever. That's why they had gotten the laptop from school in April. They hadn't been allowed to even finish the school year in person, everybody had been given a computer and told to do online classes for the rest of the school year. And they had to wear those dumb masks everywhere they went.

Levi was terrified and thought they all were going to die. Mom kept telling them everything was fine; masks and social distancing were just precautions. Abbey thought adults, especially her mom, would never tell kids the truth. Adults didn't know how strong kids really were. So, Abbey watched the local news every morning and read CDC blogs and the Journal of American Medicine's posts every day.

"It's OK. You can tell me the truth, Mom. I'm not afraid, I'm practically grown up," Abbey said.

Mom looked at Abbey for what seemed like a long time. "I know you are, Abbey. You're my big girl and I depend on you for so much. You may not think I notice how much you do around here. But, you're wrong. Without you, I don't know what I would have done. You're my rock."

When she tried to hug Abbey, Abbey drew back. She'd been dying to hear her mom tell her how much she depended on her but now that it was said, she realized she didn't want to be anybody's rock. She wanted Mom to be the rock and let her just be the kid. She knew something bad was about to happen and she wanted to run away from it as fast as she could.

"Where's Levi?" Mom asked.

"He's working on his summer reading list. I told him to go read in the bathroom so I could play music while I cleaned the kitchen. I'll go get him."

Mom stopped her. "Not yet. I need to talk to you alone. Sit down, please."

They both sat on the ratty sofa.

"I haven't lost my job but I have been sent home for two weeks. With pay. All non-essential team members were asked to take vacation for a few weeks while the bank reorganizes a little."

"Reorganize? What does that mean?" Abbey struggled to keep her voice low so Levi wouldn't hear.

"Well, you know about the virus? The reason you couldn't finish out the school year in person?"

"You said it was just a new strain of flu. You said we'd be back in class in the fall. You said everything would be back to normal in no time." Abbey knew she was whining but she couldn't help it. "What does the stupid flu have to do with your job?"

"It isn't the flu, Abbey. I didn't want to worry you. And, honestly, at first the doctors and scientists weren't sure exactly what we were dealing with."

"OK, so now they know? What does the not-flu have to do with us? Or, your job? How are we supposed to pay rent or buy food if you lose your job? What will we do?" The panic in Abbey's voice climbed with each word she spoke.

"I didn't lose my job. Not yet. Hopefully, what I do is essential enough for me to stay on even if they decide to downsize our department. There's a chance I could start working from home after my two weeks' vacation are up. And, we don't have rent anymore. Remember, we're moving into Gran's house and it's paid for. The Longstreets paid us enough for the taxes on the house this year, and if we budget, enough for utilities as well."

"How long before we can get out of here? At least at Gran's, Levi will have a yard to go play in. And I'll have a room of my own. When will they move out?" Abbey felt as if she would jump out of her skin. Her entire body vibrated with the urgency to move into Gran's immediately.

"Mrs. Longstreet has already moved to Oregon for her new teaching position. Her husband stayed behind to direct the movers. They're supposed to finish up today or tomorrow. They hired a cleaning company to go in and give the place a thorough clean after they're completely out. That'll take at least a day. So, if all goes as planned, we should be ready to start moving Thursday or Friday."

"And, this not-flu? That isn't anything we have to worry about, is it?" Abbey could hear the desperation in her voice but she was powerless to stop it.

"I believe it's much worse than they thought at first. It's called Covid and it isn't a flu. It's a very dangerous virus and most doctors think it could kill lots of people, unless we stay very, very careful. We'll have to stay home, unless it's absolutely necessary and wear masks everywhere we go."

"Even to church?" Abbey asked. Abbey relied on church for her sanity. No matter how bad things got at home, church was a safe place. She could go sit way in the back, on a pew all by herself, and let her mind wander anywhere it wanted to. She never joined any of the stupid girls' groups or youth whatever's. She wasn't a joiner. All those young people trying so hard to proclaim their individuality while simultaneously doing their darndest to be exactly like everybody else. If she never saw another girl tighten her ponytail and reapply lip gloss it would be too soon.

Their apartment was so small, she never had a moment of privacy. Not even a minute to be alone with her thoughts. Mom or Levi was always close by, breathing down her neck. She yearned for solitude. In church, she could have that. Sure, there were, technically, other people in the building, but nobody bothered her. Everybody assumed she was meditating or praying or something and they left her alone. Church was a place for personal introspection. It would be rude and unchristian to get all up in somebody's business while they were communing with God.

Her constant irritant whispered, *A place to recharge your batteries and reconnect with the Prince of Peace.*

For once, Abbey agreed with the voice. *That's a good way to put it. If only you would also do me the favor of leaving me alone while I reconnect. Didn't you get the notice about that?*

"I'm afraid we won't be going to church in person for a while, Abbey. All services will be streamed on the web. Nobody can take a chance of getting sick. Doctors believe this is spread by personal contact and by breathing in contaminated air. The governor has asked everyone to stay home until they can get a handle on this."

"How about school? We're supposed to start in a few weeks. Will they have it figured out by then?"

"There won't be any in-person school for a while, Abbey. I'm returning the laptop to your old school today. I've already contacted the new school; they'll fix up a packet of information and supplies and have them waiting in the drive-through for all parents to go pick up tomorrow. I'll have to use some of the rental payout to buy a nice computer and a printer. We'll need to have a good set-up so we all can stay connected and do our work from home. We'll all be working together from our own home. Won't that be nice?"

"Nice? No job. No school. No church. Why is this happening to us?" The part Abbey thought but didn't say out loud was, *And, no dad. Are you punishing us, God? What did we do wrong?*

God moves in mysterious ways, little Abbey. And when He closes one door, He opens an even bigger one for us to go through if only we have eyes to see it. Don't lose faith, Abbey. Faith is one of our most powerful tools.

"What if I'm fed up with living by faith?" Abbey answered the voice out loud.

"What do you mean?" Mom asked.

"It means I'm tired of being poor. Tired of being scared. Tired of being in charge of this family. I don't know, Mom. I'm just tired. I'm going to go get Levi."

"We aren't poor, Abbey." Mom stopped her before she could walk away and pulled Abbey into her arms. "As long as we have each other, we have everything we need. And, you aren't in charge of this family, I am. Sometimes you forget that."

Whatever, Abbey thought.

Abbey leaned against the doorframe in the hallway while Mom sat Levi down and told him the news. Stupid kid thought everything was peachy. All he heard was, "We're moving into Gran's in a few days and Mom will be home with us for two weeks! Hip-hip hooray!"

Must be nice to be young and ignorant. Abbey couldn't remember a time when she hadn't known what was going on. She vaguely remembered her mom and dad arguing after Gran died. Mom didn't want to tell Abbey anything about the sad state of their finances or their family, but Dad insisted that 'the kid was old enough to know the truth," to know it was Mom's fault they were, "so broke because she insisted on holding on to that old house like it was Buckingham Palace or something." He refused to lie to Abbey, he'd tell it to her straight.

And that's what he'd done. Levi was just a baby and she was five years old. That was the day she grew up, all of a sudden. No time for years of unicorns, mermaids, or fairy-tale stuff. Not for his big girl. Not for his almost grown-up Abbey. He told her the truth. The whole truth, nothing but the truth. Her mom didn't want them to have money and be happy. Her mom killed all of her dad's dreams and wouldn't let him have his way about anything. Most of all, Rose refused to let him sell that house.

He had big plans for his family. He was a good businessman but his wife didn't believe in him. She refused to support him or his plans. If she'd sell that house and turn their finances over to him, he'd have enough money to finally quit his dead-end job and start working for himself. Be his own boss. And rake in the dough. More money than they could even imagine. But, no, Abbey's mom ruined everything.

An audible sob escaped Abbey's throat. She had pushed that awful day out of her mind. Not long after ranting to Abbey, Dad had walked out the front door. He didn't take anything with him but his own self. That's it. Her dad left with nothing but his skin and the clothes on his back. She had run outside after him and fell down the concrete stairs, scraping both her knees. Mom was right behind her, crying, begging her dad to wait a minute. He didn't.

Mom had picked Abbey up and took her back up the steps to their apartment where Levi was wailing. Mom held the baby with her left arm and washed Abbey's knees and put band aids on them with her free hand. Then she picked Abbey up and walked to the old recliner, held both her children in her lap and rocked them until all three of them fell asleep.

It was dark outside when they woke up to the reality of their new lives. Mom, Abbey, and Levi were a team now. Just the three of them against the world. That night they all slept together in Mom and Dad's bed. Mom's bed now. Abbey had been so scared she couldn't stop shaking for a while. When she finally did fall asleep again, warm and snug against her baby brother, her mom's arms around both of them, she decided two things. One, she wouldn't cry ever again. At least not in front of anybody. Crying was for babies and she wasn't a little kid any more. No matter how scared she got, she wouldn't let anybody see her cry. Two, she would never forgive her dad. Never.

Chapter 5: *Cache (noun)*, A Great Amount of Accumulated Possessions

Their apartment had come furnished so they didn't really have much to move. All of their personal belongings fit into suitcases, gym bags, and a few large trash bags. All of which fit in their mom's ten-year-old minivan. When they arrived at Gran's house, Levi hopped out of the van and ran straight for the backyard. Which ticked Abbey off. He needed to do his share of unpacking their stuff but Mom told Abbey to leave him alone and let him have fun. *Don't upset precious baby Levi.*

Gran's personal belongings and furnishing, on the other hand, fit into what must surely be a very large storage unit. Their mom had to hire movers to haul Gran's belongings back to the old house. As Abbey watched load after load of furniture and boxes be deposited inside Gran's house, she quickly grew annoyed. *How much cash has Mom been laying out to pay for storage? Man! All the stuff we could have bought, all the cool stuff we could have had.*

She tried to calm down before she confronted her mom. She knew she'd get nowhere if she started an argument. She counted to a hundred (ten had never been enough of a countdown for her), and tried to sound nonchalant, "So, Mom. Those storage places are pretty expensive. It must have been tough making that payment every month. What with all of the expenses of raising me and Levi too. You sure are a good money manager."

Rose rolled her eyes. "Nice try, Abbey. I've known you all your life, you think I'm fooled by that weak attempt at subtlety?"

"Oh, Mom! You wound me to my core! Subtlety has never been my strong suit, I know that. I'm being perfectly sincere. How could we afford to keep Gran's stuff in storage for seven years?"

"Not that it's any of your bee's wax, young lady. But actually, we didn't have to pay anything for storage. Gran left us everything and I fully expected we'd move right in after she passed, but then, well, you know…"

"Dad happened," Abbey said.

"You could put it that way. When he refused to allow us to move into Mom's, I had to come over and pack everything up and you were so little and Levi was just a baby and I couldn't stop crying. Mr. Short, your gran's next-door-neighbor at the time, he passed away a few years ago, came over and helped me pack. He and your gran were widowed at about the same time, and I think he always had a thing for my mom."

"Gross. Skip that part please."

"My mother was a very intelligent and beautiful woman, Abbey. That's not gross. Mr. Short's family owned a farm on the outskirts of town with several large barns that he eventually turned into storage. His son still leases the farmland but keeps several of the barns for personal storage. Anyway, Mr. Short was pretty upset by Mom's death too. And he never really cared for your father. So, he came over and helped me and eventually took over the packing and moved everything out into one of his barns. Didn't charge me a dime. Such a nice man."

"I wasn't aware there was such a thing."

"As nice men? Of course, there are. Abbey, please try not to be so cynical about everything."

Levi ran in from outside in time to say, "Cynical. C-y-n-i-c-a-l. Adjective meaning doubtful, distrustful, believing that people are only out for themselves. Abbey's cynical about everybody except you and me. You know that, Mom. Whoa! Look at all this *stuff*!"

"Good grief, what is that smell? What have you been doing, Levi?" Abbey asked.

Mom laughed. "That's normal 'little boys who play outside in the summer,' smell. You're all flushed, Levi. How about taking a break and stay inside for a while? Go wash your face and hands. Whew! You are ripe."

Abbey and Levi were pumped to unpack all the boxes but Mom insisted they take a lunch break and then move through the boxes systematically. Mr. Short had labeled every box meticulously with which room the things inside had come from as well as an alphabetical listing of each item in each box.

Can you say, 'anal retentive'? Abbey thought. Mr. Short must have been as obsessive-compulsive as her mom.

For the rest of the afternoon Levi and Abbey worked alongside their mom opening boxes and sorting through the things inside. Mom labeled a huge box '*DONATE*' but every time she placed an item inside, Levi or Abbey went right behind her and got the item out and ran with it. Never in their lives had they seen such a mountain of goods. Partly because they had no room in the tiny apartment to accumulate much of anything and partly because there had never been money for anything except the bare essentials.

Their gran, on the other hand, apparently had loads of money and loads of space to collect a whole lotta everything. Abbey fell in love with Gran's old-school cookbook. It was called *The Woman's Home Companion Cookbook* and it was published as a fundraiser for WWII. There were hundreds of pages of foods Abbey had never heard of (potato Chantilly with chives? tomato aspic? butter sponge cake?), and information on how to set a table (formal and informal settings), or cut a layer cake. A ton of stuff Levi thought was garbage but Abbey wanted to go up to her room and devour.

She also latched on to Gran's collection of angels. Some were porcelain, some ceramic, some wooden, some metallic. There were about a dozen of them in all sizes and they were all beautiful. Nestled inside one box, Abbey found a glorious dream catcher. She wondered if Gran had made it herself or if she'd bought it somewhere. Either way, she knew the perfect place for that particular jewel was right above her bed.

Levi was fascinated by Gran's two huge, leatherbound books titled *The Lincoln Library of Essential Information.* Each book was about three inches thick and held facts and information on just about everything under the sun. Their mom told them it was like an entire set of encyclopedias (whatever *that* was), contained in one big book. One *Lincoln Library* was published in 1924 and the other in 1940. Mom said they had belonged to her great-grandmother Virginia, Abbey and Levi's great-great-grandmother, who had been a high school teacher and whose husband was a carpenter. Too many "greats," to keep up with them all.

Their great-grandpa Lowe, Gran's father, had collected snow globes from different places he had visited when he was a merchant marine. Levi was fascinated by them and took great care to place them around his room. He didn't want any of them to shatter.

By supper time they had made great progress on unpacking. The only things assigned to the giveaway box were a bunch of fake fruits and vegetables, a black ceramic Fu Dog (what the heck?), several macrame plant holders, some doilies, a collection of lighthouses from North Carolina, several bronze fish molds (kind of creepy), and various knickknacks that Abbey couldn't imagine anybody laying out cash for.

"I guess we're all a bunch of hoarders," Mom said. "I really thought we'd have a lot more charity items than this." Her children would be the fifth generation of her family to live in this house. Over the years each successive generation had been pretty good about winnowing out the frivolous frippery they'd collected and leaving only the items which had lasting value for the next gen to sort through. She was grateful for that because she and her kids had a hard time letting go of anything.

Levi laughed out loud and said, "Mom! Why would we give any of this cool stuff away? You must have had the most fun ever living in this house! Thank you for letting *us* live here, this is the happiest day of my life!" He gave her a big hug and ran up to his room to scope out his new loot.

"Race you to the top of the stairs, Abbey!" he called out to her.

"Loser! Eat my dust," she answered, passing him on the landing.

Had Rose's children seen her face, they probably would have been perplexed by the mixed emotions reflected there. She felt such shame at having deprived her family of this lovely old, quirky home. On the other hand, she was glad they appreciated it and felt they would have probably taken it for granted if she had made the decision to move in after her mother passed away. She had certainly taken her home and her family for granted when she was growing up.

"Oh, Mama, I miss you so very much," she whispered to the air around her. "And, thank you dear Lord. For keeping us safe. For giving me the good sense to hold out when Sam was so angry at me for refusing to sell this place. Please help me be worthy of all of Your gifts." Her prayer was a heartfelt one. She truly was thankful and determined to be the best mother she could be.

With an aching back and happy heart, she trudged into the familiar, old kitchen, the heart of her mother's home. She was glad the kitchen hadn't been upgraded except for new appliances when the old ones gave out and a new coat of paint every once in a while. The original heart-of-pine flooring looked like butter in the afternoon light and felt soft on her bare feet. Her great grandfather had built the double-stacked, Carolina hickory cabinets to reach all the way up to the ceiling. She placed the old aluminum stepstool her mother had used to reach the top shelves, back in the corner where it had always sat.

She ran her hands over the butcher block counter tops and thought it was time to give them a good cleaning and rub them down with mineral oil. She'd get Abbey and Levi to help her do that just as she had helped her mother. Then, when it was time for one of them to take over the maintenance of the house they'd know how to do it properly.

Abbey hadn't mentioned her preference for a cold, modern, glass and steel house even once since they'd moved in. Or complained about the old-fashioned layout and furnishings. She'd even caught Abbey checking out a website devoted to the restoration of vintage homes. Maybe her little rebel was growing up after all.

She still had over a week left of her forced vacation and she intended to make the best of it. If she pushed, she should have her family all squared away and ready for school before she had to go back to work.

She had no way of knowing that their lives were about to be changed irrevocably, and worse still, perhaps irreparably.

Chapter 6: *Affinity (noun)*, A Natural Liking or Sympathy for Someone

The lamp in Abbey's bedroom flickered on and off several times. Every time she got up to make sure it was turned off, the flickering stopped, only to begin again as soon as she laid back down. She saw the lights on in her mom's room, so she walked across the hall to inform her mom of the wonky wiring in her room.

"Hey, you. What are you doing up so late?" Mom said.

"Trying to get some sleep with the phantom light thingy going on." Abbey stood at the foot of her mom's bed. She explained the flickering lights to her mom. The lights didn't flicker in anybody's room except Abbey's.

"Well, that's odd. I'll call an electrician tomorrow. Mom had the wiring replaced and brought up to code right before she passed. The Longstreets never mentioned having any problems. But, better safe than sorry." She patted the bed beside her and said, "Have a look. I found my great grandmother's journal."

The cracked, leather-bound journal looked very old and possibly handmade. Instead of glue binding the pages together, the pages had been sewn with heavy twine of some kind. A leather strap was tied around the outside of the journal.

Mom opened the journal to the first page and held it so Abbey could read it with her. There was a handwritten dedication on the inside cover:

'This is my journal. I write it so anybody who comes after me will know what my life is like. With love, and truth, Virginia Grace Robinson, February 1918, Bryson City, North Carolina.'

Virginia Grace was Gran's grandmother whose husband, great-great grandfather Raymond, had built this very house that Abbey and Levi and Mom now lived in.

"Have you had this all along and are just now reading it?" Abbey asked. "That's weird for you. You're always all gung-ho about your family."

"Of course, I'm gung-ho about my family. You should be too. We're all tied together. I think we have memory in our DNA maybe."

"You can pick your nose but you can't pick your family," Abbey said.

"That's an ugly thing to say. I hope you don't talk that way at school," Mom said, frowning. "Anyway, I found it wrapped in linen, inside a little box at the bottom of this big cedar chest." She pointed to the large cedar chest that sat open at the foot of her bed. "Mom's cedar chest has been in storage all this time. I love this old thing. I wanted to keep it with me but you know we didn't have room for it in our apartment. Mr. Short knew how important it was to me. He made sure it would be protected from the elements and critters or whatever. He built a cedar crate to house it and sealed it up for me."

"Why cedar?" Abbey asked.

"Cedar repels bugs. And helps prevent mold and mildew." She held the journal to Abbey's nose, "Smell it? After all these years it still smells like cedar."

They both took a few seconds to savor the warm, spicey smell. Rose was transported back to her childhood when she had spent hours rummaging through the old cedar chest and playing make believe.

"Mom always kept the journal in her nightstand. She showed it to me years ago, I was probably about your age, I guess. We had to do a family history project in social studies when I was in the 6th grade. I read my great grandmother's journal and used it as reference to do my project. Got an A."

"Of course, you got an A," Abbey said. "The universe would have collapsed if you hadn't gotten an A. You're just like Levi. To the top of the class, or else!"

"Ha. Ha. And just how often in the past seven years of school have you made anything less than an A on any of your projects?" Mom said.

"That's different. You and Levi are aliens. There's nothing you can't do. I'm a regular human. Sarcasm is my only natural ability. I have to work at everything else."

Dear Journal. February 14, 1918. Today is Valentine's Day. Teacher gave all of us a card that she'd made and glued hearts and ribbons on. She must have worked for days to make all these cards as there is 13 of us in school. And how much money had it cost to buy ribbons? My sister Catherine (we call her Cat), and I only have one hair ribbon apiece because they cost so dear. I love Miss Todd and hope I can be rich and beautiful and smart like her one day. Papa said that was vanity and I was a vain girl and I shouldn't say such things. Mama smiled and told me I could be anything I wanted to be when I grow up. Mama's mouth smiles a lot but her eyes never do.

Dear Journal. February 8, 1918. You're not supposed to backtrack on your journal but I guess there's no help for it. I'm going to pretend I wrote this on February 8. Mama had to go into town to visit her doctor today. She gets powerful bad headaches and has to stay in bed a lot. When she got home she had this book with her. She hid it in her skirts and didn't give it to me till the babies was both in bed. She whispered that she loved hearing the stories I'm always making up and she told me to start writing things down and that maybe one day I could be a great writer like Miss Emily Dickenson, mama's favorite. Then, she told me it was just our secret.

She told me to be ever diligent about self-improvement as far as increasing my vocabulary (I use one of her old Spellers from her finishing school for lists of new and unusual words), and perfecting my penmanship. Ladies must teach their children these things so I must study to show myself approved in order to teach my own children one day.

I do not believe I want to have children of my own, one, or any day. My sister, Cat and our baby brother, Richard, are too much trouble for me to think on living with two such hellions of my own. Mothers are all born with the heart to love their children no matter what. I was not born with that heart. God must have given my loving-heart-part to another little girl.

Papa don't cotton much to reading and writing and vocabulary lists, especially not to poems. Boy, does he hate poems! Poems don't put food on the table, says he. But, me and my mama love poems so we read Miss Emily Dickenson and talk about what her poems might mean. Often, she tests me to see how many words I have added to my lexicon. I sure do love the way words feel in my mouth.

Mom closed the journal. "Just like Levi," she said. "I'd forgotten about that. See, I told you. We're all in each other's DNA."

"Come on, Mom. Do you really think loving words is an inherited characteristic?"

"I don't know. Maybe you should become a geneticist when you grow up and uncover the mystery of why we are who we are. Are we good or bad or smart or dumb or lazy or inspired because of our genetic propensities?" Mom said.

"Remember who you're talking to, Mom. I'm not Levi. Use English."

"Why do you do that, Abbey? Always pretend you aren't bright when you know you are. Are you afraid people will find out how smart you are?"

"Whatever. Can I keep the journal for a few days?" Abbey said. "I'd like to find out about the ancient ones who I share DNA with."

"With whom I share DNA," Mom corrected her. "And, yes, you may."

Abbey jumped up from the bed, took the journal, and turned to leave.

"Goodnight, Abbey. I love you, honey," Mom said.

Abbey gave her mom a little wave and said, "Back at you."

She forgot all about how sleepy she had been. She turned the bedside lamp on and told it to stop flickering, or else. Then, she continued reading the journal:

Dear Journal. March 15, 1918. Mama says today is the Ides of March and it's a bad luck day. She read all about that in one of the greatest writers of all times' books. His name was Mr. Shakespeare and mama went on and on about him. He hails from England, way across the Atlantic Ocean, a place I hope to visit one day.

Mama went to school down in Charlestown where her people are from. She said they had a big, white house and snow-White counterpanes on the beds. My mama and her brother and two sisters didn't all sleep together in the same bed as Cat and Richard and I do. Every one of the children in mama's household had a bedroom of their very own.

Also, according to my mama, there was always a white linen tablecloth and a crystal vase full of flowers on the dining room table. They had a dining room! Which is a room where you don't do anything except sit down at the table and eat. I tried to imagine how such a thing could be possible but I couldn't. Her people had Money and didn't like my papa much because he didn't. I love my papa and can't figure out how Money can make people like or not like you.

Our home is a three-room, shot-gun house, same as just about everybody else's around here. Although some do live in log cabins passed down to them from their people. Papa's a good carpenter so we are fortunate to have a new house that's got all the joints fit snug and no drafts come in. Papa cut trees from our lot and took them to the lumber mill to be hewn to build our house. What he couldn't make, he bartered for. Mama says they camped out on our land for almost six-months after they were first married while papa worked on building our house after he got in from the fields at night. A-course, I don't remember that because I wasn't born yet.

My mama is beautiful and good and kind and makes the best biscuits in the county (papa proudly tells everybody). My papa is what some call a character. He sings as he works and appears happy most of the time. He is also a teller of tall-tales. Which, when I was little, I took for the whole truth. I fully believed his stories about the time when he was a scout for General George Washington. I used to beg him to tell me more about the olden days when he would creep, silent as a whisper, through the woods, on the lookout for the British.

General Washington himself nicknamed papa "Whispering Wind," on account of how he never made any noise, even when he trod upon dry leaves.

I usually keep my mouth shut in school, let the girls with pretty ribbons in their hair and store-bought dresses draw attention to their selves. No thank you, sir, I don't want anybody casting their eyes upon me. But one day teacher was reading us a story about The American Revolution, that's when we became a Country on our own without no help from that rascal King George. I like to bust, waving my hand up in the air, all excited to tell the class about my papa being General Washington's right-hand-man. Teacher called on me and when I was finished shooting off at the mouth about my papa who was a famous hero, everybody in the room started laughing. Teacher told me nicely that my papa had been pulling my leg and none of his stories was actually true, in a factual way.

I cried all the way home. Papa apologized to me and told me I should a-knowed he was joshing. I reckon he truly felt bad about me getting laughed at in school. I only wish he'd a-told me he was joshing before I made a fool of myself.

Chapter 7: *Affability (noun),* The Quality of Being Pleasant and Friendly

Davis was a fourteen-year-old boy who lived down the street. He came by their house the day before their mom went back to work. He glided up the sidewalk on his skateboard and rang the doorbell holding the *POSITIV Team Complete* board in front of him like a shield. It had skulls and flames painted on it and Levi thought it was the coolest thing ever.

When Mom opened the door for him, he greeted her with a hearty, "Good morning, ma'am. My name is Davis Loftin the Third and I live four doors down from you." He turned toward his house and pointed it out to her. "I saw some kids in the yard the other day, so I thought I'd come and check it out. See if I could maybe make some new friends. The people who lived here before you didn't have any kids."

"Very nice to meet you, Davis Loftin the Third," Mom replied. "My son, Levi, is seven years old so he may be a little too young for you to hang out with. My daughter, Abbey, is twelve but I'm afraid she isn't much into skateboarding, or sports."

"Hey, no prob. I'll just wait out here on the porch if that's OK with you. I'd at least like to meet them."

"Nonsense, come on in and have some chocolate chip cookies. Abbey just made a fresh batch." She asked if he had a face mask. He patted the pockets of his jeans and said he must have left it at home.

Mom grabbed a mask from the box she kept by the front door and waited for Davis to put it on before she ushered him into the house.

Levi and Abbey were both at the kitchen counter beside the stove. The first batch of cookies had just come out of the oven and Abbey was filling up the cookie sheet with a second batch. Levi was fast-counting to one hundred because Abbey wouldn't let him eat a cookie until it had cooled for one hundred seconds.

Mom led Davis just inside the kitchen. She placed a chair by the door and told him to have a seat. "Abbey, Levi, this is our neighbor from four houses down, Davis."

"Everybody calls me, Davey," he said. "Nice to meet you Abbey and Levi. Boy, am I glad there's finally somebody under a hundred living in the neighborhood. No offense, ma'am."

Mom laughed, "None taken. I still have a few years left before one hundred. Sorry about having to seat you on the other side of the room but we can't be too careful these days. Social distancing, you know." She handed him a hot, fresh cookie. "I'll get you a glass of milk, or would you prefer juice?"

Davey struggled trying to figure out just how he was going to eat a cookie through a face mask. Mom said, "It's OK to pull your mask down while you eat, Davey. You're at least six feet away from Abbey and Levi. Just please put it back on after you finish eating."

"Yes, ma'am. Milk, if it's no trouble," he answered. "Wow! Abbey, you sure can cook! These are the best cookies I've ever tasted! They are crazy good!"

Abbey managed to mumble something that sort of sounded like "Thanks." She was mortified to have this guy sitting in her house, at her kitchen table, eating her cookies. He was gorgeous. And, he was in high school. If Drew could see her now, she'd have an absolute fit. And, she'd know just what to say. Drew was cool and could handle being around boys.

Abbey was glad to have something to do so she wouldn't have to sit down and talk to him. She stole glances at him occasionally but, for the most part, kept her eyes downcast and focused on her baking. Davis, *Davey* was tall and skinny with a shock of black hair that fell into his eyes. He had to sling it back every once in a while, so he could see. He had big brown eyes and the longest, darkest eyelashes Abbey had ever seen on anybody, boy or girl.

Once, he looked up and caught Abbey's eyes. He smiled the biggest, most beautiful smile and her heart melted. She forgot about being awkward and shy. He was so handsome he'd never, ever consider somebody like her for a girlfriend. She didn't have to worry about impressing him, she could be her ordinary self. He'd only think of her as one of the guys. There was safety in that knowledge.

After their mom thoroughly investigated him and he scarfed down half a dozen cookies, he said his mom expected him home to finish his chores and he had to leave. He asked if he could come back and maybe show Levi around the block. And Abbey too, of course. If she wanted to.

Mom assured him he was welcome any time. Just be sure to stay six feet apart and wear your mask, she reminded all of them. And, if anybody feels like they have a cold coming on, stay away from each other completely. The children all assured her that they knew the drill. Until this darn Covid thing was over, they'd all mask up and go around the neighborhood looking like bank robbers.

After Davey left, Mom said, "What a nice young man. And, his manners are impeccable. You two could learn a thing or two from him."

"Puleeesse..." Abbey wailed. "Did you have to give him the third degree? I bet he won't come back. Ever. He probably thinks this house is a police state or something."

"Don't be so dramatic. It's my responsibility to look out for my children and make sure they hang out with the right sort of people. And I was just being polite asking about his family. Show him we were interested."

Apparently, all three had been impressed by him. He was an only child. His mom was a homemaker, he said his dad called her a *domestic goddess*. His dad was in commercial real estate and traveled a lot, so Davey had to be the man around the house most of the time.

"I think Abbey's *really* interested," Levi said.

Abbey blushed a bright scarlet. "Shut up. You're an idiot!"

"Hey, watch your language," Mom warned. And to Levi. "It isn't polite to make fun of your sister. Abbey and I both found him to be quite attractive. There's nothing wrong with that. Your sister's growing up, you should get used to the fact that she'll be having boyfriends soon."

"Shut up! Both of you! I don't have a boyfriend and I never will! I hate stupid boys!"

Levi chanted, "Abbey's got a boyfriend. Abbey's got a boyfriend…"

Abbey ran up to her room and slammed the door shut. Thankful she had a room of her own and thankful the door on it didn't stick so she could slam it whenever she had the need.

Davey's father was on the couch in the living room when he got back home. *Either sleeping one off or tying one on* Davey thought. When he closed the front door, his dad sat up, shook a cig from the pack and lit it up, sucking on it for dear life. His dark hair had gone almost completely gray and his once flat belly hung low, almost to his knees. "Where you been you little cockroach?"

"Just skating around."

"Lousy skateboard crap. That's all you think about. When I was your age my old man would 'a beat me within a inch of my life if he'd a caught me skatin' around town like a big sissy. Make yourself useful, I'm starving. Get your sorry butt in the kitchen and fix me somethin' to eat."

His dad pulled his shirt up, pulled lint out of his belly button and scratched his stomach.

After taking out three cookies for himself, Davey threw the brown paper bag full of Abbey's cookies to his dad. "Eat these. I got them from down the street. You sorry drunk."

Obviously, not drunk enough to let that pass. He jumped up from the couch fast as a rattler and grabbed Davey's arm, twisting it until it hurt so bad Davey couldn't hardly stand it anymore.

"Had enough? Huh? Say it. Had enough?" His dad spit in Davey's face when he spoke. Davey wanted to cry out and beg his dad to stop but he was determined not to do that again. Showing weakness just made his dad even meaner.

Davey didn't give in to the pain and humiliation. He stood toe to toe with his old man, clenching and unclenching his left hand into a fist.

His dad shoved him down to the floor and laughed. "You little pip squeak. Think you can take me on? You ain't man enough. Never will be. Go on in the kitchen and heat up a frozen dinner or something. And bring me another beer. 'Bout time you started doing somethin' to earn your keep around here. Show me some 'preciation for all I do for you. Ungrateful pup."

When Davey fell to the floor, the mask Mrs. Whit had given him fell out of his back pocket. His dad picked it up. "What the heck is this? You turning communist on me? What are you doing with a face mask?"

"The governor says we should all wear a mask to protect us from Covid," Davey said.

His dad laughed like that was the funniest thing he'd ever heard. "Governor? Governor? I don't give a flip what that idiot says. He ain't my governor. I sure bud didn't vote for 'im. And, for your information, we ain't in Communist China, we're by-god Americans and don't you forget it. Nobody tells us what we can and can't do. It's wrote down right there in *The Constitution*. And in *The Good Book*. What? You plan on turning atheist too? What are you lookin' at? Git! Go fix me somethin' to eat."

Davey thought his father had probably never read the U.S. Constitution and he knew for a fact there wasn't even a Bible in their house. As far as voting, according to his dad, "Only suckers vote."

His father continued grumbling. Davey tried to block him out. "My own flesh and blood spouting communist mind control bull. I never thought I'd live to see the day. Ain't got the common sense God give a donkey. Where did I go wrong with that boy? You try to raise 'em right and this is what you get."

There were no dinners in the freezer. As usual, the kitchen cabinets were mostly empty too. Beer was the number one item on his dad's grocery list. And they were about out of that too. Davey guessed his dad would roust himself up and go down to the terminal in the morning to pick up his paycheck and, hopefully, a load of freight to deliver. Davey saw delivery vans and trucks everywhere these days. He knew his dad could get more delivery gigs if he wanted to. He was too dang lazy. He wished his dad would pick up a long-haul route and get out of his hair for a few weeks.

The guys down at the freight office thought Slim Jim Loftin (a nick name he'd gotten long ago because of his penchant for eating the dried beef snacks), was a swell guy who worked hard and maybe drank too hard but they couldn't fault him none for that. Didn't he keep a roof over his kid's head? And look after him all by his lonesome after that no-count wife of his up and left him high and dry? Went to see a man about a used car, took it out for a test drive, and just kept on drivin'. None of the Blanton girls was any good. They were lookers all right but none of 'em was better than alley cats. Slim Jim's wife was no exception.

Davey took the two butt-ends, the only slices left in the loaf of bread, and spread peanut butter on the crusty sides, smashed them together, and left the white bread side up. There weren't any paper towels, so he shook the crumbs off the dirty dishrag that was lying on the sideboard, put the sandwich on that. He delivered the sandwich and a beer to his dad then went back into the kitchen, got the last beer and took it down the hallway to his own room.

It wasn't long before his dad hollered at him, "Yo, commie brat! Bring me another beer."

"Sorry, you're all out. That was your last one," Davey answered. "Time to make a store run, I guess."

His dad crumpled the empty can and threw it across the living room, cursing loudly.

Chapter 8: ***Religiosity*** *(noun),* Broadly speaking, having to do with religious thoughts and beliefs within a community

Dear Journal. August 26, 1918. For a little village, hardly a stop in the road, we do surely fear the Lord, as proved by the number of churches we have around here. You can't sling a cat without hitting upon a church. When one cantankerous person (of which our community has a plentitude), or group of people get fed up with the preacher or their pew-neighbors, they just up and move down the road a piece and start themselves a new church. That's how we came to have such a heap of churches for such a small population of people.

My mama and her people are Lutheran but good luck finding any denomination that is not Baptist of one stripe or another around here. She settled on our church because she would druther be bored than take part in what she calls the shenanigans that some local churches are fond of. You see, our preacher is lacking in what you might call personality or wit. Or public speaking ability. However, he is a sanctimonious man who does not suffer fools.

The Hard-Shells call each other out, right there in the sanctuary, and take a vote to cast any member out of their fellowship who is thought to be committing grievous sin. Mama says they must of skipped over the verses that tell of Jesus saying, "Let him who has never sinned cast the first stone," because the Hard-Shells are mighty fond of stone-throwing only with their words and not real rocks.

The story goes that one Sunday, one of the Hard-Shell church brothers stood up and requested prayer for his neighbor's daughter who he said was a 'loose woman on the order of the Great Whore of Babylon'. Well, sir, being so concerned for that girl, their preacher called a halt to the service and organized a group of saints who went straight away to that poor girl's house, jerked her up off her front porch where she was shelling peas, and dragged her back to the sanctuary where her accuser confronted her. You have to give it to the Hard-Shells, they don't talk about you behind your back. They say their piece to your face.

Turned out to be a case of mistaken identity. The young woman he had seen tippling moonshine and dancing with the fiddle player at the barn dance down by the river was this girl's mama (who had married very young and looked more like a sister than a mama) and the handsome fiddler was the woman's brother from down in South Carolina.

P.S. The shine they were drinking was actually homemade Peach Brandy, which everybody knows is the accepted remedy for the croup and is in no way against any church's mandates. Lots of people start taking the croup cure early on before any croup can set in.

I believe the Hard-Shells to be the major cause of us having so very many churches.

The Snake-Handlers used to have a majority of churches around here but due to obvious reasons like people's natural aversion to the arch enemy in the Garden of Eden, people scared of getting snake bit, or worse yet, people scared of getting snake bit and dying, their membership has been dwindling in recent years. They have had to shut down all but one of their churches.

Last year, one of their members took The Great Commission to heart and set about devising a plan to increase the flock of faithful at his church. Their church roof had been patched till it was more patches than roof and it leaked profusely. But the church coffers were mostly bare. Without an infusion of new members and the cash money they would bring in, he feared the roof would collapse. As it stood, Preacher Hawkins and his eleven children made up the majority of members in that church, and as everybody knows the Hawkins have never had the talent for money-making. Or, for handling snakes for that matter. At one time or another, every one of them has been laid up or even hospitalized way over in Asheville, on account of snake bites.

This well-meaning Snake-Handler decided to sneak into our church and put our people under conviction of our sins by showing us the true path to salvation was in demonstrating one's faith in God by handling serpents without fear. How can they know lest someone teach them?

He was prepared to demonstrate the depth of his own devotion to the Lord and the strength of his beliefs by bringing snakes into our sanctuary, turning them loose during the sermon, and then gathering all of 'em up and wrestling them into a box with no harm done to himself or anybody else.

He showed up on Homecoming Sunday, carrying a basket just like everybody else, full of what we thought to be food for the supper under the trees after the service. Of course, there was no food in his basket, he'd rounded up a bunch of snakes and loaded them in his basket instead.

When he set his basket down, he jostled it a little and the snakes started slithering out and sliding down the aisle. Preacher had the deacons round up the reptiles and the "visitor," and show them the door. Mr. Sutton, the pretend visitor, should have known we would find him out, he'd been a member of our church for thirty years before he got offended by the preacher's message on tithing three Sundays straight. He figured he had no choice but to move on down the road and join up with another congregation.

He had tried out the Hard-Shells for a while after removing himself from our congregation, but was dissatisfied with their firm stand against drinking alcohol except for medicinal purposes. The Sutton's have a long-standing family tradition of making fine moonshine and he could not *abide the idea of turning his back on his ancestors. He believed the Hard-Shells were likely to hunt down his still and smash it up so over to the Snake-Handlers he went.*

Sometimes I wish I was a good enough Christian to stand in judgement of others with the Hard-Shells. Or, have the courage of my convictions and the faith to know I could handle snakes with impunity. I guess I'm just too weak.

Chapter 9: *Prevaricate (verb),* To Lie

Gran's house was twenty miles away from Mom's bank. Their old apartment was only about four miles away from her work. Because of the increased distance, Mom had been hesitant to allow Abbey to continue to be in charge of Levi. In case of emergency, she could rush home to the apartment in under five minutes. From Gran's, getting home took more like thirty minutes. She knew how important the babysitting stipend was to Abbey, but she thought Abbey was too young for such responsibility.

She and Abbey debated the question for days. Mom felt it would be neglectful of her not to have an adult babysitter with her children while she worked. Abbey insisted she could take care of Levi just as she had been doing over the summer. And she needed that babysitting money to buy a phone of her own.

Abbey laid out her arguments, penning them as well as speaking them aloud. She even posted her list on the refrigerator:

1. I have been cooking and cleaning for the past three months anyway.

2. Levi listens to me and does what I tell him to do.

3. Both me and Levi know your rules and promise to keep them.

4. Mrs. Jarvis can't drive. If Levi or I get sick or injured, the only thing she can do for us is call 9-1-1. Both of us are capable of doing that.

5. We just changed school districts. If we have to stay with Mrs. Jarvis, we'll have to switch back to our old school again. What a hassle!

6. Once school goes back to in-person learning, the school bus stop is only two doors down from Gran's house. That means we ride the bus to school and back, getting home only a few hours before you get home from work.

7. For the time being, the governor asks that everybody stay within their own family bubble. What if we get Mrs. Jarvis sick? She's so old, it'd probably kill her. Making us murderers.

8. Driving us back and forth to Mrs. Jarvis' will add hours to your day and take away quality time we could be spending with each other.

9. Mrs. Jarvis doesn't have internet. She thinks it's subversive and dangerous. So, how can Levi and I do online classes from her apartment?

Mrs. Jarvis, their next-door neighbor in their former apartment complex, was lonely since her husband died and loved having children around, even if they weren't her own. Over the summer, she had kept an eye on Rose's children, dropping in every day to visit for a while. She refused to take money for being on-call, so Rose repaid her by sharing their Friday night suppers with her. Mrs. Jarvis informed Rose that she would happily watch over Abbey and Levi again while Rose was at work, the children would just need to be dropped off at her apartment every morning.

Abbey was determined to keep the previous status quo. No way did she want to spend entire days over at Mrs. Jarvis' apartment while they did online classes. Or precious after-school hours of freedom cooped up in Mrs. Jarvis' apartment after school returned to in-person learning. In the end, Abbey got her way. She promised Mom she would be 100% responsible and no fussing with Levi and no rule breaking.

The first week their mom went back to work, Abbey and Levi fell back into their former summer routine of Abbey being in charge and Levi closeted away studying his lists of words. Now that they had separate rooms as well as a big back yard they could have their own space to get away from each other when tempers flared. And, they had Davey.

Davey made it a habit to drop by around lunch time each day. Abbey wondered why his mom allowed him to eat away from home so often but didn't have the courage to ask him. He brought his gaming console over and taught Levi how to play video games, he helped Abbey pick vegetables from the small (but mighty), garden in their back yard, and he played board games with them. He was so much fun. Time flew by when Davey was around. Abbey knew she wasn't supposed to have company when Mom wasn't home but Davey wasn't technically company, he was more like family to Abbey and Levi.

She didn't lie to her mom about how often he came around but she didn't volunteer the information either. She struggled with the notion of degrees of dishonesty. Was not telling Mom about all the time they spent with Davey actually a lie? Was it as bad as something like stealing the money Mom kept in her top dresser drawer? A thing Abbey would never do. Was there a sliding scale of sins? From one – ten, not telling Mom about Davey was no more than a two. Stealing, well that was a definite ten.

Tread carefully, Abbey, her constant irritant warned her.

Mind your own business, Abbey thought in reply. *Davey is a nice boy and I like having a friend to talk to.*

On the last day of summer break Davey burst into the kitchen and announced, "OK campers, today is our last day of freedom and we aren't going to let it go to waste." He didn't bother knocking anymore, Abbey left the back screen door unlocked and it became his habit to just walk right in. He was practically a member of the family after all.

He told Abbey and Levi to follow him, he had a secret place he wanted to show them. Abbey felt a small degree of hesitation, her mom didn't allow them to leave the yard while she was at work, but Levi was out the back door before she could remind him to put on a pair of shoes. Barefoot was the official dress code of the south during warm months, which, by the way, was pretty much most of the year.

There was a trailer park two streets over from their neighborhood. It almost looked haunted. Several derelict, rusty trailers with doors gaping open and garbage strewn across the dirt patches that made up the front lawns stood side-by-side with places that looked sad, but inhabited. Most of the trailers that looked like people lived in them had huge dogs staked and straining at the chains that secured them, growling and barking as the children passed by.

Without realizing what he was doing, Levi took Abbey's hand and held onto it until they passed by the trailer park and entered the woods behind it. Davey didn't seem to notice the children's discomfort. He picked up the pace and led them into the piney woods.

They walked for about five more minutes when Levi tugged at Abbey's hand and whispered, "I think we should go back home."

Davey looked back at his friends and said, "Don't wimp out on me now, my man. Almost there."

He led them on for another few hundred yards. Finally, the undergrowth flattened out and they were on a barely discernable foot path. He pushed weeping willow fronds aside to reveal a circle of clear, flat ground overlooking a deep gorge with water swirling over rocks and sand bars.

"How did you ever find out about this place?" Abbey said. It seemed so isolated from their neighborhood they could be on another planet. There were no sounds of humanity. Just bird song and the noise the rippling water made. Shafts of glittering sunlight cracked the clouds above the gorge and made what Abbey thought could be chutes up to heaven itself. She wondered if maybe this was what the Garden of Eden had looked like.

"I come here all the time when I need to think or just get away from it all. Here, have a seat Abbey." Davey pointed to a tree stump that sat in the middle of the clearing. Then he moved to stand on the edge of the precipice overlooking the gorge. He closed his eyes, threw his head back, and windmilled his arms as if he might attempt to fly.

"Are you out of your mind? That's dangerous! Get back here!" Abbey cried. She jumped up from her seat and started to make a dash for Davey to pull him back. Levi stayed frozen in place on the stump, watching in horror.

Davey laughed. "Chill. You can't go through life being afraid of everything." He walked back toward Abbey and Levi. He pulled a loose cigarette and a book of paper matches out of his shirt pocket, and lit up.

He held the lighted cigarette out to Abbey, "Here, take a hit. You aren't afraid, are you? How about you, Levi? Sneaking off to smoke is a rite of passage. Sooner or later, everybody does it."

The siblings were too stunned to speak. Finally, Abbey said, "Your parents let you smoke?"

Davey laughed. "Of course not. What would be the fun in that? I swipe cigs from my dad all the time. Long as I only take one or two, he doesn't know. And what he doesn't know won't hurt him. Or me."

"What. Are. You. Talking. About?" Abbey yelled at Davey and stood up, pulling Levi up with her. "And, for your information, Levi has asthma pretty bad. Did you forget about that? Smoking could kill him. Come on, Levi. We're going home."

Davey tossed his cigarette on the ground and followed. "Hey, wait a minute. Don't get mad. I just wanted to have some fun."

Suddenly, Levi screamed out and fell to his knees which made him scream even louder. He had stepped on prickly Sweetgum Tree burrs. His feet and knees were covered in them. Abbey and Davey both knelt and began to pull them off Levi's skin. He was sobbing so hard he lost his breath.

"Where's your inhaler?" Abbey demanded.

"In... *uhhh... whoop*, my... *uhhh... whoop*, bedroom, *uhhh... whoop*," he managed to answer in between gulps of air.

Davey scooped Levi up, threw him over his shoulder like a firefighter might do, and took off running. When they got to the street Davey turned left instead of right. This was a different route than the one they had taken to get to Davey's hide out.

"Where are you going? I need to get him home!" Abbey was frantic.

"Short cut," Davey said.

Abbey's constant irritant was calm but forceful. *He's hyperventilating. Steam. Get him in the bathroom and use steam to help regulate his breathing.* Abbey didn't bother questioning the voice, she followed its orders.

She had Davey take Levi into the powder room downstairs and told him to turn on the hot water faucet in the sink. She ran upstairs into Levi's room and grabbed his inhaler off his dresser.

She told Levi to use his inhaler, then, she grabbed a towel, put it over Levi's head and instructed Davey to hold Levi up with his head hovering over the faucet. She knew Levi wouldn't be able to stand on his own with burrs still attached to his feet. She rubbed his back and whispered that everything would be OK. "Just stay calm, Levi. Doesn't that feel better already?"

Within a few minutes under the towel-tent, Levi's breathing gradually returned to normal. Davey eased Levi down onto the commode seat and Abbey turned the water off. Levi's eyes were swollen and red-rimmed from crying. There were rivulets of dirt rolling down his cheeks. Abbey had seen Levi have an asthma attack before but never one as bad as this one.

She went back upstairs to get her mom's tweezers from the makeup bag Mom kept on the vanity in her bathroom. While she knelt, using the tweezers to pull the tiny spikes from Levi's feet, Davey used the blade of a knife he pulled from his jean's pocket to get the remaining burrs out of Levi's knees.

"You carry a weapon too? Jeez, what else don't I know about you?" Abbey was furious.

"It isn't a weapon, Abbey. It's a Swiss Army Knife. Everybody has one."

"I don't. Mom will be home soon. You need to go. We aren't allowed to have company in the house while she's at work. And we aren't allowed to leave the yard. She's gonna kill me."

"You're going to *tell* her? Are you crazy?" Davey said.

"No. I'm honest. And you need to leave."

"Please don't be mad at me, Abbey. You're the best friend I ever had. I'm sorry Levi had an asthma attack. I didn't know. I... I guess I didn't think. I made a mistake."

"Your 'mistake' could have gotten my brother killed. It was stupid for me to go along with you. This whole thing is my fault. Please leave."

As soon as Davey left, Abbey told Levi to go upstairs and get in the bathtub. She started the water for him while he got out clean clothes. Her butt was itching like crazy. She wondered how mosquitos had been able to bite her under her clothes.

With Levi in their bathroom, she went into her mom's bathroom and dropped her shorts so she could inspect the bites on her back side. *Not mosquitos. Chiggers.* That darn tree stump must have had a nest of them. She knew she'd be itching for a week. She found a bottle of calamine lotion and dabbed it all over her inflamed behind. She called out to Levi, asking if he was itching anywhere. Of course, he was.

She took the bottle of calamine, placed it on the floor by the bathroom where Levi was, and told him to put the lotion on everywhere it itched before he got dressed. As an afterthought, she got a pair of long pajama pants out of Levi's bureau and took them to the bathroom door. She told him to put on long pants. She hadn't exactly decided to lie to Mom but she thought she needed to plan a coverup (literally), just in case she had to.

The coverup is always worse than the crime, her inner voice chided her.

Didn't ask for your input, Abbey thought back to the hateful irritant. She knew she could count on Levi to keep his mouth shut if she asked him to. She was so close to having enough money for her own phone and today was her mom's payday. She thought it unfair to jeopardize the phone she'd worked and saved so long for just because of one stupid mistake.

Lying to your mother is one thing. Lying to yourself is another.

I don't have time to deal with you. Mom's probably on her way and I still have to put supper together. So, just shut up! The voice had become so loud and clear Abbey wondered if maybe she was losing her mind.

Mom was late getting home from work. The streets around their neighborhood were blocked by fire trucks and police cars. Somebody had set fire to the woods on the block behind their house. They watched the local news together that night. The fire marshal believed the fire was a result of either carelessness or had been intentionally set.

Because of the current drought conditions, he said once the fire started it didn't take much for it to become a dangerous, full-blown inferno. Campers may have been careless with their campfire and when it began to spread, had gotten scared and ran. Or, there had been a malicious actor with no regard to the destruction they had caused.

Residents who lived in the mobile home park that bordered the burning acres had been evacuated from their homes and given stipends to spend the night in a local hotel. Firefighters positioned themselves between the mobile homes and the wildfire in an effort to protect private property. By seven-thirty p.m., officials believed the fire to be 90% controlled and expected all residents to be able to return home the following morning.

Anyone with information about who may have started the fire was urged to contact the fire department or city police.

Abbey and Levi stared straight ahead, neither spoke.

Chapter 10: *Charlatan (noun)*, A Phony

After their mom left for work the next day, Abbey and Levi avoided making eye contact with each other as they sat on opposite ends of the dining room table doing their online classes. Both of them realized how close to disaster the previous day had been. Actually, for many families (both human and animal), it *had* been disastrous.

For Levi, the most egregious sin had been lying, by omission, to his mother. He valued her opinion of him more than just about anything and he feared she would think less of him for lying. He was still reeling from the news story about all of the small animals that had been displaced because of the fire. Firefighters had even found several animals dead because they couldn't escape the smoke and flames in time. He felt responsible for all of those deaths because it was his asthma attack that had caused Davey to throw down his lit cigarette and carry Levi back home.

Abbey was most concerned about losing the privilege of being in charge of Levi and the house on the days Mom worked from the bank. Because of Covid, the bank was experimenting with different work location scenarios in order to keep their employees safe and socially distanced from each other and their clients. A fully staffed, bustling office was no longer considered ideal. Currently, Mom was alternating working one week from the bank and one week from home. She was pretty sure she and most of her colleagues would be asked to work exclusively from home sooner rather than later as Covid cases in their area continued to rise.

If and when the time came for Mom to work exclusively from home, Abbey would lose her babysitting and housekeeping money, which worried her greatly.

She was doing some research on the flu of 1918 for her social studies class. Doctors were saying Covid was sort of like the 1918 Spanish Flu pandemic which infected over 500 million people around the world and killed over 50 million before it was done. If Covid became as horrible as that earlier pandemic she knew her reign as wage earner would soon be over because all three of them would be quarantined together at home for a very long time.

When they did their family devotionals every night they always sent up special prayers for all of the doctors, scientists, and medical caregivers around the world. They asked God to grant those workers the wisdom and skill to care for the sick and dying and to find a cure for this virus before it became as deadly as the 1918 one.

They also requested patience for their fellow citizens who, like their own family, were so scared and so used to having immediate resolutions to all their problems, they couldn't deal with the situation they found themselves in. They heard stories every day about people getting into arguments or even fights with friends and neighbors. Mom said she believed, in their hearts, most people are good and kind. But, fear and uncertainty can turn people ugly.

People with medical problems like asthma were thought to be in greater danger than those with no underlying conditions. Mom fretted over Levi constantly and wouldn't allow either Abbey or Levi to go grocery shopping any more. She did all their shopping alone, took all the bags out of the car, then placed them on the back porch, sprayed then down with disinfectant, and waited for them to dry before she brought them inside. The ordeal slowly evolved into a normal ritual, one that was observed by families all over the nation. Just life as we know it in these modern times.

Sometimes Mom had to go to several different places to find supplies. Shelves in even the biggest stores were often emptied within an hour of the store's opening. Toilet paper was a precious commodity. As was disinfectant of any kind and hand sanitizer. Abbey and Mom were OK eating meat but now that stores were always running out of chicken and beef, Levi's vegetarian preferences were fortuitous.

When they finished with their schoolwork for the day, Abbey made peanut butter and jelly sandwiches for lunch. Levi brooded over his sandwich, so Abbey had to force him to eat even one bite. She finally persuaded him to eat by promising him they could pick flowers from the backyard, take them to the woods and scatter them around for the lost animals, as soon as he finished eating.

Abbey's usual modus operandi was to act first, ask forgiveness later, but with so much on the line she decided to play it by the book this time. She called their mom and explained how upset Levi was about all the displaced and dead animals from the fire and how much it would soothe him if they could take some flowers over and do a little service for the animals. Mom gave them permission to leave the yard but told Abbey to be very careful and go straight over and straight back and call her when they got home safely. Abbey didn't mention the fact that she'd already told Levi it would be a good idea. Baby steps on the new and improved Abbey.

She made Levi wear his mask, just as Mom had asked, even though they were outdoors. Abbey didn't feel the need for that precaution since it was unlikely they would pass anybody out walking but she did it anyway to appease Mom.

When they got to the fourth house below theirs, down at the cul-de-sac, they saw a young mother coming down the sidewalk from the house holding the hand of a toddler girl and pushing a pink stroller with a sleeping baby inside. Obviously taking the kiddies out for a walk but how could that be? Davey said he was an only child. He never mentioned anything about two baby sisters.

Being careful to keep a safe distance away from the woman and her children, Abbey put her own mask on and called out, "Hello! We live four houses down. I'm Abbey and this is my brother, Levi."

"Very nice to meet you, Abbey and Levi. I'm Yvonne and these are my daughters, Gracie and Faith."

"Are you, by any chance, Davey's mom?" Abbey said.

"I only have the two children," Yvonne answered. "I don't believe I know any boys on this street named Davey. Before the outbreak we used to do neighborhood cookouts and gatherings here in the cul-de-sac; I can't recall meeting a boy named Davey. You and your family recently moved into the Longstreet's house, didn't you? I apologize for not coming over to meet you yet, but, well, you know... Covid."

"Yeah, we know. It's nice to meet you. I hope we can get back to having neighborhood things again. Have a good walk," Abbey said.

Levi started jumping up and down like he was about to pee in his pants. Abbey knew what he was dying to say, so she interrupted him before he could spill the beans about that particular house and urged him to keep moving.

"But, but, Abbey that's Davey's house. How can that not be Davey's house? We've passed it a dozen times when we were walking with him and he always gave the house a salute as we passed by. Why did she say she didn't even *know* Davey? I don't understand."

"No. But I think I do," Abbey said. She picked up the pace and within only a few minutes they stood in front of the Bel Aire Mobile Home Court, the trailer park that bordered the woods. The stench of smoke was heavy in the air, it stung the children's eyes and nose. There was yellow crime scene tape strung around the shells of trailers that were completely or partially burned. Acrid smoke was still rising off the burned husks of trees in the background.

They both stopped abruptly when they saw the lone figure sitting on a rickety picnic table with his back to them. He was drinking a soft drink straight from the two-liter bottle, a half-smoked cigarette hung from his left hand. He was barefoot and more unkempt than usual. He burped loudly and wiped his mouth on the sleeve of his dirty tee shirt.

"Nice," Abbey said. "Although I'd think you'd want to cut back on smoking after all the damage you did here yesterday."

Davey jumped, dropping the soda bottle in the mud at his feet. The caramel-colored liquid fizzed and foamed as it spewed out of the bottle. His startled expression gave Abbey all the information she needed to confirm her suspicions.

"Abbey! What are you two doing here? I was just on my way to come see you. I decided to swing by here to make sure all was under control so I could report back to Levi. Are you doing OK today, my man?"

"He's not your man and he isn't OK. Look around you. People lost their homes. Animals died here last night, Davey. And you're sitting there smoking? What's wrong with you?"

"Whoa. Chill. It was an accident. And, I'm as sorry as you are. I didn't start the fire on purpose. Why are you giving me such grief? You're worse than my mom."

"Speaking of your *mom*, Davey. We saw her leaving *your house* just now, with her two daughters. And, she never even heard of you. Pretty crappy excuse for a mom."

"I can explain," Davey said.

"Whatever. Every word out of your mouth is a lie. You only pretended to be our friend. You don't know the meaning of the word."

"Abbey, please listen to me. Let me explain. I know I lied about where I live. I was skating by your house that day and saw you and Levi and your mom going in your house and I thought how great it would be to be a part of a family like that. So, I hung around outside for a while working up the nerve to ring your doorbell. I never meant to lie to you. It just sort of happened."

Levi wiped tears from his inflamed eyes and said, "But you lied to us, Davey. Friends don't lie to each other. Is Davey even your real name?"

"Of course, it's my real name. Duh. I'm not a spy or something stupid like that."

Abbey said, "Which one of these is where you actually live?"

"That would be this gem right here," he said, pointing to the rusting trailer he was sitting in front of. It rested on cement blocks. It was brown in some places, silvery colored in others. The front door was wide open, a faded purple and green striped bathroom towel was duct taped over the three diamond-shaped windows in the door. The steps leading to the front door were made of rotting wood pallets stacked haphazardly. "Would you tell anybody you lived in a place like this if you were me?"

"I've never been ashamed of my family or our home. I've wished we could have had a big house and money for stuff we couldn't afford but I've never lied about where I come from. Mom says *poor* is a state of mind," Abbey said.

"Bravo for Mom! She obviously never went to bed hungry because the fridge in her *state of mind* was completely empty. And, compared to this piece of junk, you live in a mansion. If you knew I lived in a place like this you'd never have spoken to me. None of you. Your mom wouldn't have let me in the front door."

"If you believe that, you never knew us at all. And I feel sorry for you. Not because of where you live but because of how you think. And, for your information, we lived in a stinky, old tiny apartment all our lives. It had two bedrooms the size of postage stamps and shaggy, brown carpet. Mom didn't buy the house we live in now. It's our grandmother's house. Gran left it to us after she died. I love our house and I know how lucky we are to have it. But without our grandmother we wouldn't have it."

"At least you had a grandmother who had something of value and she cared enough to hold on to it and pass it along to you. I come from a long line of losers who don't pass anything down from one generation to the next except dirt and misery. And alcoholism, can't leave that one out. Drinking yourself to death is a long-standing family tradition." Davey squeezed the tip of his cigarette out between his thumb and forefinger then placed it carefully in the bottle cap which rested beside him on the picnic table.

"Are you really an only child?" Levi asked.

"As far as I know. There could be some half-sibs somewhere. My mom took off when I was five. I have no idea where she is or what she's doing. Not being a loving mother to anybody is a pretty safe bet. My old man could have some brats scattered around somewhere. Don't know. Don't care."

"That's disgusting. Come on Levi, we have to get back home before Mom calls to check in on us," Abbey said.

"But, the animals. And the flowers..." Levi whined.

"We'll put these flowers in a vase for Mom and pick more later for the animals. I promise, we'll come back. It's just too late today. Mom deserves flowers from us after all we've done. Actually, she deserves a lot more than what she's been getting from us. We, *I've* let her down and I'm ashamed of myself. She deserves the truth."

"We're going to tell her?" The pitch of Levi's voice climbed higher with each word.

"Yes, we are. Holding out is the same as lying so we're going to do the right thing. Tonight. No more lying. Even if it means I'll never get a smart phone, I'm through with lying."

Davey jumped on that last statement, "So, you're saying it's OK for you to lie to your mom but I'm a horrible person because I lied to you? What if I just come clean like you plan on doing tonight? Huh? Will that make me OK again? I just told you the truth about my life and you're still passing judgement on me. I'd say you're a big, ole hypocrite, Abbey."

"And, I'd say you're right, Davey. I'm sorry I lied to my mom and I'm going to tell her so and ask her to forgive me. And she will. Eventually. She'll ground me for a few weeks. Or months. But, she'll get over being mad at me. I think. Mostly, she'll be disappointed in me. I can't tell you how crappy that makes me feel. I've been a smart aleck for as long as I can remember but I've never lied to her. I don't know how long it'll take her to start trusting me again. This whole thing sucks." She took Levi's hand and turned back toward home.

"How long before you start trusting *me* again, Abbey? If I give you my word I'll never lie to you about anything again? Will you trust me again? Can we be friends again? Hey! This sucks for me too," Davey said.

"I'm sorry, Davey. I don't know. I just don't know." Abbey wasn't sure why she was so hurt by Davey's lies. She certainly understood why he was ashamed of his home, regardless of what she told him about never having been ashamed, herself. She knew because she'd felt that way plenty of times. That's why she'd always insisted that her birthday parties be held in a park or a fast-food place, somewhere away from home. She didn't want everybody in her class to look down on her or feel bad for her because of her obvious poverty.

For some reason, Davey was different. She expected more of him than she did of herself. She knew it wasn't fair, knew it was a double standard, but it was how she felt. Her mind was a jumble of unintelligible emotions. She decided she'd wait till later to try to sort them out. Maybe talk it over with her mom. Mom always had pretty good advice, for a mom, that is.

Oh, what a tangled web we weave when first we practice to deceive.

Not you again, she thought back at the constant irritant. *Maybe I'll tell Mom about you and she'll take me to a psychiatrist who'll say I'm crazy as a loon and lock me away forever and keep me drugged so I'll never have to listen to you again.*

Not a chance, answered the eternal voice.

Chapter 11: *Infirmity (noun),* Sickness

Abbey set the dining room table for supper that night, putting the flowers in a vase in the center of the table. She was a nervous wreck. She worried about losing Davey's friendship; she was already starting to feel bad about yelling at him. And she worried about how Mom would react when she heard the truth about Davey spending so much time inside their house and their long walks exploring the neighborhood. She was pretty sure she'd lose her weekly allowance.

She was thankful for Gran's beautiful dishes and cutlery and for a home that had a true dining room. Just touching the lovely old dishes calmed her down. Being in this house, surrounded by all the hand-me-down items made her feel like she had a connection to her gran and all the great-grands who came before her. She wondered how people get to be wise and if it would ever happen to her. She was a collection of bad decisions and poor choices.

She practiced what she would say to her mom. She didn't want to just blurt out, "I've been breaking all the rules you set for me when you allowed me to be in charge while you were at work." Levi helped out by suggesting words when Abbey got stuck on what to say next. Living with a pint-sized genius had its perks.

Mom got home a little early, carrying her laptop and a small box of items from her work cubicle with her. The bank had decided everybody in Mom's division would work from home for the foreseeable future. When Levi ran to hug her, Mom pushed him away. "I'm feeling a little under the weather, sweetie. Don't want you catching any of my germs."

Abbey took the laptop and box from her mom. "I'm sorry you aren't feeling so good. Maybe if you take a hot bath and get into bed you'll feel better. There aren't many things a bubble bath won't cure."

Mom stopped midway up the stairs, shook her head, looked back at Abbey, and said, "What did you say? Where did you hear that? For a minute I thought you were my mother. You sounded just like her. She used to say that to me all the time."

"I don't know why I said it. It just occurred to me, that's all. Mom, are you OK? You really don't look good."

"I'm fine. Just a little tired. Think I'll take a nap." Then, she collapsed on the stairs. Abbey managed to catch her mom's head before it banged on the landing. She held mom's head in her lap and ordered Levi to go get a pillow off the couch so she could place it under Mom's head. She called her mom's name over and over but got no response.

Abbey was numb. She felt as if she were in a trance or maybe having the worst nightmare imaginable. Levi was sobbing and screaming at her to do something.

"Shut up for a minute! Your yelling isn't helping at all. Stay back. You heard Mom, she doesn't want you around her in case she has germs."

Abbey walked back down the stairs on rubbery legs. She found Mom's cell phone in her purse and called 9-1-1.

"She has it, doesn't she? She has Covid. She's going to die and we'll be all alone and she'll be dead. She'll be dead. Abbey, what will we do? She can't die. God won't let her die, will He?" Levi was shouting at her.

"She isn't dead and she isn't going to die. Just please shut up, Levi. Go to your room and read some words or something while we wait for the ambulance."

"I'm not going anywhere. I'm not leaving my mommy. Mommy, please wake up! Please!" He hadn't called her 'mommy' since kindergarten.

Abbey was as scared as he was but she knew better than to let it show. If she lost control, she knew Levi would probably have a total nervous breakdown or something. For his sake she had to pretend she wasn't terrified. She could feel her body spasming so hard she felt as if she might just fly apart. She had never imagined fear could be such a visceral experience.

Mom started moaning and tried to sit up. Abbey ran up to her. "Don't try to get up, Mom. Just lie still. Help is on the way. I called 9-1-1, they're sending an ambulance."

"Ambulance. No need. I'm fine. Help me up. I just need to lie down. Where's the baby? Mama, do you have the baby? He's crying. I think I'll just lie down for a minute," Mom was talking out of her head.

Abbey couldn't see through the curtain of tears streaming down her cheeks. *She thinks I'm Gran. Dear God, please don't let her die. I'm sorry I lied. I'm sorry I let you down. Please take me instead of her. I'm the one who deserves to die, not her. Levi needs her. Please. God.*

She heard the ambulance pull into the driveway and ran to open the door. "Here! She's in here! She just fell down and I can't get her to wake up. Please hurry!" She ushered Levi out to the front porch so he wouldn't get in the E.M.T.'s way.

The medics revived Mom but found she wasn't able to answer their questions, so they turned to Abbey. They wanted to know everything that had happened and an exact timeline of events since their mom got home.

After doing a ton of paperwork, they tore off the carbon copies and gave them to Abbey. They told her they were taking her mom to City Memorial Hospital and she could call the emergency department there later for an update on her mom's condition.

A policeman, who had arrived shortly after the paramedics, came inside to talk to Abbey. He asked if her dad was home and if not, was there was somebody he could call to come over and stay with Abbey and Levi until their dad got home.

Bile rose in Abbey's throat and she went cold with an inexplicable fear. Sweat popped out on her forehead and from her arm pits. She'd watched enough crime dramas on television to know what happens to unsupervised children. Nothing good. Just when their life was finally starting to become as she had so long wished for, she teetered on the brink of losing everything.

"No. Our dad's... gone. I mean he's away. He isn't here. He's still at work."

"I don't think it's a good idea for you and your brother to be here alone," the officer said. "We need to call your dad at work and have him come on home. He needs to know what's going on."

"He... travels. He's a delivery man. You know how everybody gets stuff delivered to their homes these days. He's always on the road so we really can't call him right now." Abbey's brain was going ninety miles an hour. She knew it was obvious she was lying and feared what the policeman would do if she couldn't come up with something convincing to tell him.

"He doesn't have a cell phone?" the policeman asked.

Abbey couldn't think of anything to answer that, so she remained silent. She could hear Levi out on the front porch. He had stopped crying and had the hiccups.

"I'm afraid I can't leave you and your brother here alone, honey. I need the name of an adult I can call so we can get somebody over here to stay with you until your dad gets home. Or, I'll need to call the county so they can send somebody."

"My... my Gran. My grandmother. My mom's mother. We call her Gran. This is her house. She lives here with us. I mean, we, we live here with her."

"Where is she? We need to talk to her before we can go."

"I'm not sure. I think she's up in her room. She goes to bed real early because she's so old."

The officer looked closely at Abbey. Then, a door closed at the top of the stairs. He straightened up and said, "Sorry, ma'am. I didn't see you standing there. I'll leave my card with your granddaughter. If you folks need anything at all please don't hesitate to give me a call. I'll do what I can."

Abbey watched in fascination and disbelief as her grandmother nodded to the police officer and said, "Thank you for your kindness, officer. The children and I will be fine."

Abbey turned slowly to the officer to try to judge whether he had seen and heard her grandmother or not. Was there such a thing as group hallucinations? He wrote a phone number on a business card and handed it to her. "Here you go, young lady. This is my personal cell phone number. In case you need me. I'm real sorry about your mama but I'm sure she'll be right as rain in no time. Try not to worry."

Abbey pulled Levi in off the porch and shut the door behind the policeman. She asked Levi if he saw anybody standing up at the top of the stairs. He said there wasn't anybody left in the house but the two of them, so how could somebody be upstairs? She risked a glance back at the stairs and saw there was, indeed, no one there. Cold chills ran up and down her spine.

Don't wimp out on me now, little Abbey Rose. You've got to keep the faith baby.

"I'll try my best," Abbey said to the empty space above her. She told Levi it was supper time and led him into the kitchen where the food she had prepared for Mom was still out on the stove.

This time she didn't bug Levi about not eating. Neither of them had an appetite. They were both sick with worry about their mom. Levi helped her clear the table and put the food away in the fridge. She loaded the dishwasher and turned out the kitchen lights. She led Levi back to the dining room and said, "We have to talk."

Levi started in crying again and Abbey had to threaten not to let him talk to Mom if he didn't get his act together. She used her mom's cell phone to look up the number for the hospital's emergency room, then she placed the call. The lady at the information desk said their mom was in the Emergency Department but she had no information about her condition. She took down Abbey's cell phone number and the landline number, and promised that somebody would give them a call back as soon as possible. If nobody called within the next few hours, Abbey was welcome to call back.

"Who'll come and take care of us?" Levi asked. "That paramedic told me the police would send somebody to stay with us until our dad got home. Our dad's never coming home, Abbey. So, who will the police send to take care of us? I want to go see Mom. I want my mom."

Abbey considered herself a pacificist and was kind of surprised at the swift violence of her reaction to Levi: she grabbed him by the shoulders and shook him, then immediately regretted it. "You have got to get a grip, Levi. Why are you acting like you're three years old? We can't go see Mom now. Maybe not for a long time, it depends on what's wrong with her. If she's contagious we won't be allowed to see her at all. At least not for a long time."

"I'm too little to live by myself. And we can't drive. How can we go see her when she's better if we can't drive? I'm scared, Abbey. I'm so scared. I'm trying to be brave but it's too hard."

Abbey put her arms around her little brother. He was so thin she could feel every bone in his back. He hugged her and they cried together for a long time. They knelt down right there in their dining room and prayed like they'd never prayed before. Surely, a just and loving God wouldn't take their mother away. Leaving them orphaned.

But lots of children were orphaned every day, weren't they? Abbey knew that but for the grace of God, she and Levi could have been in an even worse situation. They were no more loved by God than any other children around the world. She had no right to expect her lot to be dramatically better, different than children in developing nations. The problem was far too complex for Abbey to come up with a rational conclusion or explanation. All she could do was plead. *Please. Please. Please.* She knew God would fill in the words her brain couldn't come up with.

"I'm scared too, Levi. And, I'm sorry I shook you. That was wrong and I'm so sorry. But we're going to be OK. I know we will. Even if Mom has to stay in the hospital for a whole week, we'll be OK. We've been by ourselves for a whole week while she was at work. We can just pretend she's at work and do what we usually do."

She told Levi to get a notebook and pens from the makeshift classroom in the dining room and meet her in the kitchen. They needed to plan their strategy for getting by until Mom got back home. Word lists calmed Levi down. Making lists calmed Abbey down. She needed the calm that writing lists, organizing her mind, made her feel.

She turned the kitchen lights back on and saw Davey standing by the back door. She had forgotten to lock it. She also forgot how mad she was at him. When he spoke to her, she melted and began crying again. *Haven't cried in years and now I can't stop. I'm pathetic.*

"I'm so sorry about your mom, Abbey. Please don't cry. I'm sure she'll be OK."

"How did you know about Mom? How long have you been here?"

"The whole time, I guess. I wanted to see you again, try to talk to you, but I was afraid to come in, so I rode my board around the block a few times, trying to get up the courage to come and see you. Then when your mom got home, she sort-a struggled getting her stuff out of the car. She dropped a bunch of stuff and I picked it up for her but she acted like she didn't know who I was. That was spooky, so I decided I'd better stick around. I've been waiting in the backyard for a while. I was going to go on home when I saw the lights in the kitchen come back on. Just wanted to make sure y'all were OK. I'll be going now."

Abbey told him he didn't have to leave. She was still mad at him but she appreciated his concern and, honestly, she could use a friend. She got down three bowls and filled each with chocolate ice cream. Levi came in with the pen and paper, saw Davey, and ran to hug him.

"Our mom's sick, Davey. They took her to the hospital. Me and Abbey's all by ourself. The police said they'd be back to check on us but they didn't get here yet."

"I know, Levi. And I'm sorry 'bout your mom. But the cops not coming back is a good thing. You don't want the cops coming back to check on you."

"But why?" Levi asked.

"Because they'll call Child Protective Services and take you away from here and put you in a group home or foster care. They'll separate you and Abbey," Davey explained.

"He's already scared to death. You didn't have to tell him that," Abbey snapped.

"What? You want me to lie to him? He's smart Abbey. And he's old enough to know the truth. He needs to know what's at stake here."

"Is he telling the truth, Abbey? Is that why you lied to the policeman and told him dad would be home soon? The police are our friends, we have to tell them the truth," Levi said.

Davey harumphed at that but Abbey shushed him.

"The police *are* our friends, Levi. But, they're also adults and they have tons of rules they *have* to follow. No matter what. I didn't want to upset you more than you already were. It's enough to have to worry about Mom. I didn't want you to find out that if they knew we were all alone they'd rip us apart. But you really don't have to worry about that. I'll never let anybody break us up. Never."

"Neither will I," Davey said.

"Neither will I!" Levi said. "I'm not a baby, Abbey. I'm sorry I got so scared. But, I'm OK now. And I know our mom will be OK. If God can protect Shadrach, Meshach, and Abednego from the fiery furnace, He can protect us and our mom. Consider the lilies of the field…"

Abbey couldn't help herself, she laughed out loud. Then, Levi joined in. Abbey explained to Davey that that was one of Mom's favorite Bible quotes, she was always saying it to them when they got bent out of shape worrying about Santa Claus making it to their house when they were so broke or about not having enough money to pay the cable bill. Mom was big on considering the lilies. That verse meant God was in charge, so His children didn't need to be worrying about anything. It just sounded weird to hear Levi quoting their mom. And it felt so good to laugh again.

Abbey put a spoon in each dish of ice cream and told the boys to have a seat. "We've got plans to make. Lucky for us, this Covid thing has turned the whole world upside down. I guess 'lucky' isn't the right word. I just mean the world is a different place now than it was a few months ago. I'm not sure all the old rules still apply."

"Do you think our mom has Covid? People are dying from that every day. And, if she dies, we'll never be allowed to stay here. I thought I was brave but I don't think I am," Levi said.

"Yes, you are," Abbey said. "You're brave and you're smart and you know all about keeping the faith, baby. That's an old hippie saying, Gran told me about it. And Mom is definitely not going to die. She'll be back home before you know it."

"School won't be a problem because nobody's in school in person anymore. That's a huge plus," Davey said.

"That's right. All of our classes are online, so we'll just keep doing our schoolwork like we have been. When Mom has to sign any paperwork or anything we'll just sign her name electronically like she's been doing anyway. Our teachers won't know the difference," Abbey said.

"You'll need to let her work know she's sick before they fire her for not showing up," Davey said. "She'll probably keep getting paid if she has sick days left for the year. But you'll have to do a crap load of paperwork for that," he paused to consider the best course of action to take. "Maybe it'd be better not to let them know. You don't want them snooping around here."

Abbey thought about that for a few seconds then made a decision. "Nobody's going door-to-door to check on anything while Covid's around. Everybody's scared of everybody else. We'll have to tell her boss she's sick and in the hospital. I'll call her friend Sherry at work in the morning. Then we can email her manager. If we can figure out how to get into Mom's work computer, she'll have his email there in her contacts. Levi can write out the message so it'll sound like it came from a grownup with a corncob stuck up their butt and I'll sign Gran's name on it so Mr. Gowers will think Gran is here with us."

"I don't know, Abbey. We just made a promise never to lie anymore. It seems like we're starting to be career liars," Levi said.

"This is an emergency situation, Levi. We won't lie any more unless it's an absolute emergency. Emergencies change the rules. Isn't that so, Davey?" she asked.

"Works for me," Davey said. "And I know a thing or two about lying. Sometimes you just have to. To protect yourself. And, I had to go to foster care one time after my mom left. I was crammed in a room with four other kids, all of 'em crying all night. It sucks. If lying is what it takes to keep you here at your own house, then lying is definitely the best policy."

"Under normal circumstances lying is bad. Heck, under any circumstances. Lying is wrong. I know it's wrong but I can't think of another way to keep us out of foster care, Levi." Abbey knew she'd have to come clean eventually. Especially if Mom, if Mom… jeez, no wonder Mom refused to say the word "died," It was just too painful. Too final. She would never accept the fact that Mom could die.

"How are you set for food?" Davey asked. He couldn't remember a time when he wasn't hungry and he didn't want his friends to go through that, even for a day.

"We have a garden that's still producing out back. And a freezer with stuff in it. And, everybody orders food online these days. Every grocery store in town delivers for free because of Covid. We can order the things we need and use Mom's credit card to pay for them online. We can do the same with Levi's medicine at the drug store."

"How will we get to the hospital to visit Mom?" Levi said.

"We'll call for an Uber or something. Quit making up problems. We'll take every day as it comes," Abbey said.

Davey said, "We'll need to do something about your mom's car."

"What about Mom's car?" Abbey said. "Why would we need to do anything about her car?"

"The neighbors all saw your mom being taken away in an ambulance, Abbey. So, they know she's in the hospital. None of them will chance coming over here to look in on you because everybody's too scared about catching Covid. But they still probably wonder what happened to the two kids who live here. Maybe you haven't been here long enough to make friends with any of your neighbors, but somebody's bound to start making some calls pretty soon," Davey said.

"We don't know anybody here," Levi said. "I don't think anybody even knows we live here. Nobody goes outside hardly any more."

"Miss Yvonne. She knows we're here. The lady who lives down in the cul-de-sac? We talked to her; she knows about us. She was really nice. But she's a mom, she'll want to make sure we're OK," Abbey said. "How will doing something with Mom's car help us keep Child Protective Services away from us?"

"We want the neighbors to think your mom got sick but she's OK and everything is normal around here. We have to make them think your mom's back home and back at work. So, early every morning, we can drive your mom's car around back by the gardening shed. Then, in the evenings, we can drive it back around front and leave it sitting in the driveway."

"You do know that none of us can drive?" Abbey reminded Davey.

"Maybe none of *you* can drive. I've been driving my dad home from bars since I was ten years old. Nothing to it."

"I'm not so sure about this, Davey. I think we should take a vote. All in favor of moving Mom's car raise your hand," Abbey said.

Levi and Davey both raised their hands.

"You can't vote, Davey. This isn't your problem," Abbey said.

"I'm your friend and the only one of us who can drive so I say my vote does count. Leave the keys hanging by the backdoor as usual. I'll come by at six every morning, get the keys, and move your mom's car. That way you have an alibi."

Levi corrected him, "Not an alibi, Davey. Plausible deniability."

"Whatever, young Einstein. You really do read dictionaries, don't you?"

"A 'course I do. You knew that. You really think Mom has Covid, don't you? There's no cure. She could die." Levi started in crying again.

Abbey scolded him. "Levi, it's time to practice what we preach. We say we believe God loves us and takes care of us. If we truly believe that, then no matter what happens we'll always be OK. The next few days may not turn out the way we want them to but that doesn't mean God isn't still in control. We'll do our part and He'll do His.

Keep the faith, baby, Abbey's constant, and suddenly very welcome, inner voice repeated. Abbey realized exactly who that disembodied voice belonged to. *I should have known.*

"It's been you all along," Abbey said out loud. That annoying, constant irritant had actually been her grandmother's voice.

"Huh?" Davey said.

"It's been me doing what all along?" Levi asked.

"Not you, Levi. Gran. Gran is here with us. Here in this house. Sometimes I can hear her voice. And I can feel her presence. Haven't you ever felt her?"

"I don't know. I don't think so. What does she feel like?"

Abbey rolled her eyes so hard it hurt. "You are so freaking literal."

Chapter 12: *Metaphysical (adjective)*, Beyond the Laws of Nature

When Abbey was satisfied with the plans they had made, she wrote everything down. Her beloved lists. They kept her on track. Calmed her nerves. Never having been in this situation before, she figured they had probably not thought of lots of details but she'd just add them as needed.

Levi begged her not to make him take a bath but she reminded him they had agreed to go about their lives as if everything was normal. "Besides, when Mom gets home and asks us how we've been we are not going to lie to her about anything. She makes you take a bath every night so I'm going to make you take a bath every night. End of discussion."

Levi stomped upstairs and slammed the bathroom door shut. He was usually so timid, that was quite an act of rebellion. Abbey smiled. Levi would need to toughen up a lot if they were going to get through this nightmare.

You really do sound like your mother, the voice said.

"Did you hear that?" Abbey asked Davey.

"Hear what? I don't hear anything but the water running in the bathroom upstairs," he answered.

"My gran's voice. I can hear it in my head. You think I'm crazy, don't you?"

"No. You told me your gran was born in this house. And she died out in the backyard. I guess there's probably still some of her *whatever* roaming around here."

"Life force. Her life force is still here. Yeah, I think that's it." All of a sudden, she felt bone tired. "Thank you for being here for us, Davey. But, it's really late. Your dad will be wondering where you are. I think you need to go on home now."

"Yeah, my dad's big on worrying about me."

"Davey, can I tell you something and you won't freak out or think I'm bonkers?"

"I will never think you're bonkers, Abbey. What is it?"

"This is so hard. No way to sugar-coat it."

"So, don't. Just say it."

"Tonight, when the police and fire department were here I… I saw Gran. Standing up at the top of the stairs."

"Cool," Davey said.

"Cool? Really? I tell you I saw my dead grandmother and all you can say is 'cool'? That's not all. I heard her speak out loud. The policeman who was here saw her too. And I think he heard her speak. She thanked him for his concern and told him we would be OK."

"How do you know he saw her? Or heard her?"

"He responded to her, Davey. He looked up, saw her standing there, and tipped his hat to her. Then he handed me his card and told us to call if we needed anything. That's when she thanked him. I heard her say, 'thank you, officer.' Sometimes I think I'm actually crazy. I see people who aren't there and hear voices nobody else can hear."

"You just said the policeman heard her. And saw her. Even if he didn't, *you* did. You're always trying to get me to read the Bible and believe the things it says. You say you believe. If that's true, then, well, *believe*. Believe in magic or miracles or whatever it is you say you believe in. If you believe it, then it must be real. That's good enough for me."

Then, he leaned in to Abbey and kissed her.

"Don't forget to leave the screen door unlocked and the car keys on the peg by the backdoor. See you tomorrow."

She'd never kissed anybody before. Her heart was pounding a million miles an hour. She was suddenly tongue-tied. She couldn't say anything, so she just waved goodbye to Davey. She wished with all her heart her mom was here so she could talk about this with her.

She climbed the stairs like a sleepwalker. Levi asked what was wrong with her when she came in to check on him. She just shook her head, too afraid of what she might say if she opened her mouth.

After taking a bath, she called the hospital again to see if there was any news about Mom. The emergency room nurse said Mom had been transferred to the Covid Unit. Abbey's heart sank when she heard that. She got the number for that unit and called. The phone rang so long Abbey thought maybe she had misdialed but just as she was going to hang up and try again, a lady answered.

Abbey identified herself and asked about her mom. The nurse was sorry to tell Abbey that her mom was on a ventilator and couldn't talk.

She took Abbey's number and told her she'd call back as soon as she could. If Abbey had a smart phone (since she now had Mom's phone, she did), the nurse promised to do a video call so Abbey could see her mother. Abbey thanked her and hung up.

This isn't fair, she whispered. Then she threw the stupid phone across the room. *Great, you big dummy,* she scolded herself. *Now you've done it, if you've broken Mom's phone you won't be able to see her when the nurse tries to do a video call.*

Abbey berated herself mightily while she struggled to put the two halves of Mom's phone back together without being able to see very well because she was crying so hard the tears blurred her vision. No need to pretend she'd never cry again in her whole life. Obviously, tears were her new norm. She knew her plan to save her brother and herself from foster care was dumb. How could she outthink all the grownups in town? She was just a stupid kid. Her Mom was going to die and she and Levi would be raised by idiots in some lousy group home. Her life was so miserable she thought she should just lie down and die.

The walls of her room seemed to be crowding her out, she felt stifled. She ran down the stairs, out the kitchen door, and into the back yard. Finally, she sat on the stone bench under the magnolia tree and cried out to heaven. "Why are you doing this? What have I done that's so bad you have to punish my whole family? I give up. You win. Take me. Take me and leave my mom and my brother alone."

"You've always been melodramatic. Your mother was when she was a young girl too. And, to be perfectly honest, I have to admit I had a streak of melodrama in me as well. I guess it's a family tradition." Her gran had joined Abbey and now sat, smiling and serene, beside her on the bench.

"You aren't here. I'm hallucinating. Or I'm just insane," Abbey said.

"Then why are you talking to me?" Gran replied.

"Maybe I'm dreaming. Are you a dream?"

Gran answered, "Do you think I'm a dream?"

"No. I think I'm crazy."

"Good. Now that we've got that out of the way, I have something to show you. Come along." Gran got up and walked toward the rose bushes. "Oh, how I love yellow roses. My grandmother planted these bushes fifty years ago. She created this particular hybrid and called it 'Janey's Nightgown'. A good southern lady knows her birds and her flowers. Your education in those matters is severely lacking, you should remedy that."

"I'll get right on it. Where are we going?"

"Here," Gran answered.

"The backyard? Why are we…" before Abbey could finish that sentence, she realized she had been transported somewhere that was still her backyard, but, at the same time, *wasn't* her backyard. Or, maybe the *location* hadn't changed at all. Maybe it was the *time* that had changed. She felt calm, swaddled in peace. She smelled hot chocolate and clean clothes that had dried outside in the sunshine.

Her mind was flooded with visions of her own past. She remembered there had been a clothesline, secured to a metal pole shaped like a "T" on top, here in this backyard. She had a vision of herself as a little girl, helping Gran pull the wooden clothespins that held bed linens to the clothesline, putting them into a little paisley-print bag Gran kept tied around her waist when she hung laundry. Abbey was so little she fit in Gran's big wicker basket and Gran let her jump in on top of the laundry. She remembered thinking she could just melt into the clean sheets because they smelled so good. They smelled like clean, fresh sunshine. How about that. Sunshine was something you could smell?

It was dark in this place, but there were millions of tiny twinkling lights glowing all around her. Maybe not lights, more like clear gemstones that shone with light from within. She could hear a sound like wind rushing all around her but she didn't feel any wind. The sound of the wind grew louder and was joined by what sounded like water, like waves crashing on the shore.

She had never felt happier in her life. She felt safe and… loved? Yes, loved. She was swaddled in deep blue love. "Where are we? What is this place?" she asked Gran.

"Hmmmm, words are so limiting, ideas are more comprehensive. Everyone has their own name for it, I suppose. I call it 'The Mom Cave'. I'm not sure it has a proper name. It's a place I thought you needed to visit tonight. You've been here before but you don't remember. As we grow up, we all forget the blissful hours we spent in this place."

Abbey laughed. "I'm sure I would remember if I'd ever visited here before. How could anybody forget this? You call it 'The Mom Cave'? That's not a very celestial name. Not nearly fancy enough."

"I'm not a fancy kind of person, so, no fancy names. Levi would call it something much grander. Utopia Planitia I believe he once said."

"Levi has been here?" Abbey asked.

"Of course. Listen, what do you hear?"

"I hear the wind all around me. Which is weird because it doesn't feel windy. And, I hear the ocean. But I can't see the ocean."

"That's because you're listening with your ears. Close your eyes and listen with your heart."

A skeptic by nature, Abbey didn't think it would make any difference but she closed her eyes anyway. "Whatever it is you're trying to tell me, you need to just come out and say it. I'm really not in to all that touchy-feely-kumbaya stuff. *Whoa,* what just happened?"

With her eyes closed, Abbey looked around (Exactly how could that work? *Close* your eyes and *see*?), and saw that she wasn't in a dark place with millions of twinkling lights. She was in a place of perfect light; the light was so bright it should have blinded her but it didn't.

She slowly turned in a circle, trying to take it all in. Rows upon rows of receptacles made of multi-faceted diamonds, each filled to overflowing with what seemed to be living crystals, ebbed and flowed all around her. The floor under her feet shone with the brilliance of a hundred suns. She felt encased in a cashmere blanket of pure joy.

She could *feel* the light pulsating all around her and through her. The light was alive and she was a part of it. The rushing wind wasn't wind, it was voices. Millions and millions of voices. All whispering things she couldn't make out.

"What are those voices saying, Gran? What are they talking about?"

"They're praying, Abbey. This is the sound of every mother's prayers for her children. All of the desperation and hurt and hope and faith and joy and unconditional love of every mother who has ever lived since the beginning of time."

"How can that be? How can love or emotion be something you can hear? I don't understand."

"Maybe because you still think with your mind instead of your heart. If your mind needs something concrete to grasp, consider this: what is the first law of thermodynamics? Remember that from science class last year?" Gran said.

"Energy is neither created nor destroyed? It can be changed but not just wiped out? I never understood that at all."

Gran smiled. "You don't have to understand something in order to believe it. You don't understand how electricity works but you believe that when you flip a light switch the light will come on. What do you think happens to all the energy of a mother's prayers for her child? Does it just vanish?"

"I never thought about it. It's just words. After we say them they're gone? I don't know."

"Prayers aren't *just words*. Prayers carry all the power of the faith and hope of whomever is saying them. They never die, Abbey. They take on a life of their own and join with all the other mothers' prayers and live forever here, in this place which is an extension of our hearts and souls. The prayers grow stronger as each new prayer is added until they sound as loud and vibrant as the great wind you can hear all around you. All the love of all our mothers is added to the power of this place to create a force in the universe that is unequaled. Pure, profound, selfless love."

"And, the ocean? What is that?" Abbey asked.

"Tears. The tears of our mothers. Tears your mother has wept for you and Levi. And I've wept for your mother and my grandchildren. The power of our mothers' tears doesn't ever fade away either. They don't evaporate into nothing. They live here forever. All of our mothers' love and prayers and tears are alive and working. Joining together to soothe and comfort and protect our children."

"But bad stuff still happens. Mom might die. And your prayers for her are still here, right? Love and prayers must not be enough, Gran."

"Ultimately, we have to accept that bad things happen in each of our lives. God gave people free will and people mess up in all kinds of ways every day. But, if we only believe in the power of love and goodness, we can tap into it and use its great strength to support us and help us get through the hard times in our lives."

"Where is this place, Gran? How can this exist? It can't be real."

"Why would you limit God to something your mind can conceive and an engineer can build? He *spoke* creation into existence. His powers are as far beyond our comprehension as we are from an amoeba. Further. As far as the east is from the west."

"How can I find it when I need it?"

"This place has always been a part of you, Abbey. It's inside of you. It's always been inside of you. When you need it, you can tap into it. Draw strength from it," Gran said.

"But how? This is so, so unbelievable," Abbey whispered.

Gran whispered in her ear, "You know the answer. Every good and perfect gift…"

Is from God, Abbey thought. *Of course. All things are possible. Why did I forget that?*

Abbey opened her eyes. She was in her bed. She didn't remember coming upstairs and getting into bed. She remembered being in the garden with Gran. That entire episode must have been a dream. She threw back the covers and got up to go pee. At the foot of the bed, her sheets were wet and covered in grass.

Chapter 13: *Zeitgeist (noun)*, The Spirit or Mood of a Particular Time in History

Dear Journal. August 24, 1918. Papa left at first light to haul a load of lumber over to the mill near Asheville. Mama had to tear off a strip of her petticoat to make him a mask to wear over his face because that's the law nowadays, everybody has to cover their face with a mask out in public. Like bank robbers. A mask over your face will keep you safe from the Spanish Flu. I think maybe that means the flu bugs are scared to look you square in the face? Papa is not happy about wearing a petticoat mask, I can tell you.

He won't be back for another week or two as he's looking for work and will take anything that's offered while we wait for the late cotton crop to be ready. Mama's confinement is about over, it's time for the newest chick to make his appearance in our family. Papa promised he'd be back in plenty of time to see the new one pop out and until then, I will be a big girl and help my mama. That's not much different than usual, I told myself. Of course, I couldn't ever say such a thing out loud unless I'm hoping to get my Hide tanned. Children are to be seen, not heard. That's the law of the land in this family and always has been.

Baby Richard (who is about to be dethroned from his position as the baby), is starting to pull himself up and try to walk. We're all hoping he'll walk before the new baby gets here for it will be pretty hard to tote two babies everywhere. Of course, there's not much of anywhere to go to any more since the sheriff declared The Spanish Flu is here and everything's shut down for two weeks so's to halt its progress. After the two weeks is over, the question will be pondered by the men in charge and when or if to reopen anything will be determined.

If we had a library in town and if I could get to it, I'd sure love to study up and learn how an invisible bug can travel clean across the globe and kill so many people. It just doesn't seem possible. Lots of people say it's not possible and the sheriff's just pushing his weight around. Mama says the sheriff has enough to worry about without making stuff up and I need to clam up and stop asking so many questions.

Mostly people (and of those people, most are of the male variety), are mad at having the sheriff telling them what to do. Mama says mountain men are stubborn and contrary and can't abide anybody trying to Lord it over them. So, when the sheriff shut down the churches for two weeks, because the doctors and health department told us we needed to stay away from each other as long as that flu-bug was making the rounds, you'd a thought he asked for the head of their first-born child! Even the backsliders who hadn't darkened the threshold of any church in years, all of a sudden started clamoring for all the churches to open up and for the sheriff to be run out of town on a rail.

I asked mama what's wrong with men and she answered, "I could make you a very long list."

Dear Journal. September 3, 1918. Yesterday was a day to test our faith if ever there was one. Round about suppertime mama started moaning and grabbing ahold of her stomach. She had to take to her bed because she couldn't stand up straight.

I fixed her a bowl of cornbread and milk but she took one bite and threw up all over herself. That made her cry. She is fastidious to a fault and cannot abide being untidy or unclean in any way. I told her please don't cry mama, it's OK. Then I fetched her petticoat (now about four inches shorter than it was before she used it to make a mask for papa), and laid it over her while I scrubbed her nightgown for her. In addition to believing cleanliness is next to Godliness, mama is also modest. As she says all ladies are to be. Nobody other than a little baby should go around naked, even inside their own home. I knew that even in great pain as she was, mama would suffer embarrassment if I left her laying there uncovered.

We've got a break from the cold snap and are having some fine days of Indian Summer, so it didn't take mama's gown long to dry after I spread it out over the mountain laurel bushes out in the yard. When I brought her gown in and went to help her put it back on, her head was lolled over and I couldn't get her to open her eyes or talk to me.

I have never been so scared in all my life and I yelled out to God to please stop punishing me. And then I had to ask forgiveness because I didn't want to be the cause of my mama dying. I feared God would punish me for blasphemy and take mama.

I finally got mama to open up her eyes a little and take a sip of water. She told me to go get help, the baby is coming. Then she screamed and a torrent of blood flooded out all over her bed.

The closest neighbor we have is Miss Eugenie and her older sister Theodosia who are both old as dirt. I grabbed Cat's hand and put Richard in the wheelbarrow and took off for the sisters' house. Both of the babies were squalling up a storm and I couldn't get them to hush. I told them not to be scared because our mama was going to be just fine and we're going on a little trip like our papa.

My knees were knocking and my stomach felt like it was boiling. I had to stop the wheelbarrow and throw up before I reached Miss Eugenie's. Being a brave grown-up is sometimes too hard a thing to do.

For an old lady, Miss Eugenie sure did think fast. She told me to bring the babies inside and told Miss Theodosia to watch after them until she returned. Then, she told me to run on down to Doctor Miller's house and fetch him. I told her, Doc Miller is an animal doctor and a drunk and she slapped my face and told me to step lively and no more sass. She headed off toward our house like her hair was on fire.

Doctor Miller's house is about a mile from Miss Eugenie's. I am the fastest runner in my school. I can even beat most of the boys in a foot race which mama doesn't like me doing for young ladies don't go off racing boys. I put in my best speed and reached his house in about twenty minutes. I told him what was going on and he didn't even think about it, he got his medicine bag and told me to hop in his car.

I have never been in an automobile before and I shouldn't have been excited to do so now, what with mama in a precarious condition, but my curiosity got the better of me and I marveled at the power and speed of the machine. Doctor Miller promised to let me ride along with him sometime but I know mama and papa would never allow that to happen on account of him being a drunk and a man of ill repute regarding running with loose women in town.

Miss Eugenie had mama's bed cleaned up and changed when I arrived back home with the horse doctor. She told me to take the bloody bed clothes outside and put them in the wash tub and scrub them good and hang them out to dry on the hedges. I scrubbed them with lye soap until my hands bled but never could get every bit of blood washed away.

It wasn't long before I heard a baby crying and that was a mighty joyous sound. I went back inside and introduced myself to my new baby sister. Mama named her Rose after her favorite flowers. Baby Rose is just pure magical. Mama let me hold her and I thought she was the most beautiful thing I'd ever seen. She was prettier than the porcelain dolls in the Sears-Roebuck catalogue that Cat was always pining for.

Miss Eugenie told Doctor Miller to drive me back down to her house and told me to stay there and help Miss Theodosia with Cat and Richard. She said she'd stay and nurse mama for a few days because mama was too weak to do much of anything. Nobody questions Miss Eugenie when she bosses them around. She went to Seneca Falls, away up in New York, a place I surely do want to visit, and met with the suffragettes back in the days before I was born. She also belongs to the Woman's Temperance League so, of course, the men folks avoid her at all costs. The ladies mostly tolerate her, I think, because she is a spinster. They bless her heart and shake their heads and thank God they have husbands to keep them on the straight and narrow.

Instead of aiming to teach school, I think maybe I'll be a Suffragette when I grow up. I'm not real sure what all they stand for but I like the idea of a lady who dares to speak up to a man! That is not the way of life anywhere that I know of. Even the rooster's in charge of the hen house. I believe I'd like to try a life where ladies believe themselves to be the Men's Equal.

Chapter 14: ***Ablution***s *(noun),* The Act of Cleaning Oneself

After a few days Abbey told Davey not to move Mom's car back and forth anymore. She never was comfortable with moving it in the first place. According to news reports a lot of people were working from home so she saw no need to pretend Mom was still going into an office somewhere. If any curious people drove by and noticed the car always parked in the driveway, they'd just think everybody was quarantined inside.

People were scared. Since nobody who'd ever been through something like this was alive anymore, everybody was afraid they'd get sick and die from something invisible. It seemed like the whole country was holding its breath. Just waiting.

There was no way the kids could get into Mom's work computer, that idea was a bust. Abbey quickly found out it was encrypted and if she tried to guess passwords she'd get locked out and the FBI or somebody would show up at their door to arrest whoever was trying to access a bank computer. That made her plan to email Mr. Gowers a moot point. She couldn't find his email on the bank's website, so she finally decided she'd have to risk calling him. He was a busy executive, surely he wouldn't take the time to find out if somebody was taking care of her and Levi. She just didn't want her mom to get fired. She had to do something.

She and Levi wrote out a script for her to read. She tried to think of all the questions Mr. Gowers might have for her and come up with good answers. Mom had been in the hospital for ten days. Abbey had called her mom's friend from work and told her about mom getting sick but that was over a week ago and nobody from the bank had tried to contact them at all. Mom might be fired already.

She put Mom's phone on speaker so Levi could listen in. Mr. Gowers was kind but distracted. He had a lot of business to take care of and spending time talking to a distraught twelve-year-old wasn't exactly in his wheelhouse. He told Abbey he'd get the necessary paperwork "from H.R. and shoot it her way ASAP.' She would need to 'get her mom's P.C.P. to fill out HR 187, then the hospital docs to fill out form HR39-TM63 and then have it notarized and remit to H.Q. within the next ten days." He wished her well and told her to call back any time, it had been a pleasure speaking with her.

"So, what does that mean?" Levi asked.

"I have no idea. I guess we'll try to figure it all out when the forms get here. We need to log on to our classes now. We'll talk about this later, maybe during our lunch break."

"Abbey, I'm scared. What if we can't do this? What if Mom d… dies? What will we do? I can't do this any more!"

"You stop that cry-baby stuff right this minute, Levi Raymond Whit. Our mother definitely *is not* going to die. You know why? Because she's a fighter. She's always fought for us because she loves us. She goes to work every day whether she feels like it or not and she pays the bills and she sings songs with us and plays games with us and tells us everything will be OK even when we whine and complain about stupid stuff like a new phone and she would never give up on either of us, so *we are not going to give up on her*. Never!" Abbey was shaking and crying but, she realized, she wasn't afraid anymore. She actually believed what she was saying.

Levi put his arms around her and said, "You sound just like Mom. I love you, Abbey. I'll try not to be scared anymore. I know you'll take care of me."

"We'll take care of each other, Levi. That's what families do."

"We have the best family, don't we, Abbey?"

"You bet, squirt. Now, quit dawdling. Time for school."

The school day flew by, as it always did. The good thing about doing online classes, in addition to being, duh, at home, was they only lasted about one third of the time a full day of in-person classes would. Abbey insisted they both stay put at the dining room table and finish up all of their homework before they called it a day. No putting off any work for later. Levi made a sign that said, THOU SHALL NOT PROCRASTINATE, and taped it to the window behind the dining room table.

They had a firm appointment with their mom's nurse, Miss Robin, whose shift began every night at 7:00. She told Abbey to wait until 7:45 to call so she'd have time to get checked in and make sure all her patients were OK. Abbey started thinking she might want to be a nurse too. Something that helped people who really needed help.

So far, they hadn't been able to actually talk with their mom but they could see her and she was able to wave at them. She was all hooked up to tubes and machines and looked so tiny and almost alien. The first time they saw her, both Abbey and Levi were terrified and couldn't stop crying. But Miss Robin assured them their mom was strong and responding well to treatment. She told them the best thing they could do for their mom would be for both of them to be brave and strong, so Mom didn't have to worry about anything except getting better.

They both had to do book reports for school, so they were a little late getting to supper. Abbey just heated up last night's mushroom fettuccini so that didn't take long. Levi only ate a few bites, jumped up from the table and yelled, "Gotta poop!"

"Too much information," Abbey informed him. "That is so gross. Can't you just go without announcing it to the world?" She tried to stop him before he slammed the door on the little half bath downstairs. Because...

"Abbey! No paper!"

"Tell me something I didn't know," she yelled back at him. They were down to their last roll of toilet paper. Currently that roll was parked upstairs in Abbey and

Levi's bathroom. She had ordered toilet paper over a week ago but that item was "temporarily out of stock." Everywhere. She'd tried their grocery store, Walmart, Amazon, even their drug store. Toilet paper shortage would be funny if it wasn't actually happening.

She raced upstairs, got the paper, and rushed back downstairs where she placed it outside the door to the hall bath. They still had one roll of paper towels, which were also on back order. Holy guacamole, what was it with people and paper products? Could there really be a shortage or were weirdos hoarding the stuff? Either way, the result was the same. Abbey had stopped using paper towels in the kitchen. She still had plenty of laundry detergent, so she was using dish towels or even regular towels to clean up messes. When the last piece of toilet paper was gone, they'd have to switch to paper towels.

"Sorry, Abbey. I tried to use it sparingly." Levi came out of the bathroom and looked down at his feet, embarrassed.

"You used it all?" She wanted to scold but what was the use? Of all the dumb things to yell about, toilet paper was at the bottom of the list. "It's OK. No big deal. I'm sure our order will be here any day now. Until then we use paper towels. You have to remember not to flush 'em though. Take a plastic grocery bag with you to the bathroom and throw the paper towels in that then take it straight outside to the garbage can. I will not carry your poop for you."

She couldn't believe she was having this conversation. Seriously. The world was becoming a strange place. She thought maybe nursing wasn't for her after all. Nurses probably had to deal with bodily functions all the time. Yuk.

At seven-forty-five p.m. they called Miss Robin. Abbey thought Levi maybe had a crush on her. She was so pretty, well, what they could see of her was pretty. She was all covered in hazmat gear but her voice was soft and caring and she just seemed like she would be as beautiful outside as she was inside. Tonight, their mom was sitting up in her bed and they could see her face. Hooray! She still had tubes and scary-looking stuff hooked to her but they could see her and she could talk!

"Oh, my precious babies." Mom broke down into tears when she saw them on the phone's tiny screen. She was hoarse and her voice was barely a whisper.

"Don't cry, Mom. We're both OK. Please don't cry," Abbey said.

Miss Robin told Mom that her kids had called faithfully, every night, and they assured her that all was well at home. Their grandmother had everything under control.

"Grandmother? What? Abbey, what's going on?" Mom said.

"We're doing just fine here in our *grandmother's house*, Mom. And all of our school is online and we have the homeschool set up going. Everything's good. We just miss you. And we love you."

"I love you so much, Mom. I can't wait till you get home," Levi said.

Mom started coughing and Miss Robin told the kids that was all for tonight and to take care and she'd talk to them tomorrow.

Hearing Mom's voice was wonderful. Seeing her in that condition was frightening.

"Let's celebrate Mom's recovery," Abbey said. "We can bake cookies or brownies. Which would you rather do?"

"Can we eat them tonight?" Levi said.

"Absolutely. Whatever we bake we can stay up late and eat and we can sleep in our clothes and get up just in time for school in the morning."

"No bath tonight?"

"Nope. We talked to our mom and the world is a beautiful place and tonight we're celebrating," Abbey said.

"Brownies it is!" Levi said.

Levi acted like skipping a bath was as good as Christmas. Whatever. Abbey was tired of being his surrogate mother. Let him stink up his bedroom for one night. As long as she didn't have to sleep in the same room with him any more, she really didn't care. Tonight, they'd both be happy.

She got out a box of brownie mix and a pan. Levi danced around the kitchen while she prepared the mix and got it into the oven. He stopped suddenly and said, "Uh, Abbey. Mom's car's gone."

She wiped her hands on a dishtowel and ran to the back door, throwing it open so she could see the garden shed out back. Sure enough, the car wasn't there.

She went to the dining room and looked out that window. The car wasn't in the driveway either. She raced back to the kitchen and checked the peg by the back door. The keys were gone.

She picked up Mom's cell phone and called Davey's number. No answer.

"Do you think Davey took Mom's car somewhere? Why would he do that without asking? You don't think he took it, do you Abbey? Maybe we should call the police. Maybe somebody stole Mom's car."

"Shut up so I can think," Abbey snapped. *I am going to kill you, Davis Loftin. If I ever find you, that is. You stupid jerk. Why did I ever trust you? Gran warned me.*

Headlights shown through the dining room curtains. Levi and Abbey both ran to the front door. Davey was pulling in the driveway in Mom's car.

"You idiot! You stole our car! How could you? What were you thinking? You idiot," Abbey yelled at Davey as soon as he got inside and she closed the front door.

"You can thank me later," Davey said. "Ta-Da!" He held up a roll of toilet paper. "I risked life and limb and possible police encounter to drive all the way to Charlotte to get this precious gift for my lady fair and best bro. What? You're mad at me? Seriously?"

"Seriously. I am furious with you. You've done some really stupid stuff but this is the stupidest thing I can imagine. What were you thinking? You drove to Charlotte? Did I tell you, you're an idiot? You are an absolute idiot."

"Hey! I thought you'd be happy. You've been moaning about toilet paper for a week. I thought you'd be happy. I guess I was wrong," Davey said.

"You think? Duh. Davey, you are fourteen years old. It's illegal for you to drive. You stole a car and drove it to Charlotte? You are an idiot. I can't believe you'd do something so completely, utterly…" She couldn't think of another word to describe it.

Levi chimed in to help her in her search for the perfect word. She'd already used "idiot" several times. "Stupid?" Levi said.

"Yes. Completely and utterly stupid. Thank you for stating the obvious, Levi," Abbey said.

"I thought you'd be happy. Calm down. I didn't steal your mom's car. I used it to go find toilet paper. I'm the one who risked getting caught. Not you. Why are you so freaking mad? I don't get it," Davey said.

"Obviously. Thank you for the toilet paper. Give me the keys. Now, go home. And please don't come back while my mom's in the hospital. I knew we weren't allowed to have company in the house if she wasn't home. I should never have let you come over when she isn't here. This is my fault. Thank you for the toilet paper. It's late. Levi and I have to take a bath and get ready for bed."

Levi piped up, "But, you said…"

"Shut up, Levi. Goodnight, Davey." Abbey walked behind Davey all the way to the front door then closed it behind him and locked it. She turned out the porch light and turned to Levi, "I think I burned the brownies, I'm sorry. I'll clean up this mess and make more tomorrow."

"But I don't have to take a bath, right? You said so."

"I changed my mind. You stink. Go take a bath while I clean the kitchen. I'll be up behind you."

"It's not fair. We were having fun," Levi said.

"Tell me about it," Abbey said.

Chapter 15: *Serendipity (noun),* Something Unexpected and Happy

Abbey wasn't exactly snooping when she opened the cedar chest in her mom's room. Mom had told her how much she'd loved the cedar chest when she was a little girl. She had spent hours unpacking it and playing with the treasures inside. It had smelled so good then, and to Abbey's surprise, it still smelled wonderful.

It was full of marvels. Abbey took her time, savoring every second as she pulled item after item from the chest. There were bundles of letters tied with ribbons. She set those aside for another time. She decided to read them after she finished reading Virginia's journal. Maybe investigative journalism was a career option for her? She thought her natural curiosity would make her good at it.

There was a set of teacups and saucers that looked like they'd been hand painted and were so thin and fragile Abbey was afraid to even touch them. There was a yellow silk kimono, carefully wrapped in tissue paper. She wished her mom was there to tell her the story of that garment. Velvet bags tied with ribbons held medals of some kind. *Definitely investigate these later,* she thought.

Later that day she had Levi come outside and help her in the garden. The tomatoes were dwindling down, the cucumbers were mostly gone, the asparagus had maybe one more week left, but the okra was still growing like crazy. Their freezer was pretty small and almost completely full of their summer's vegetables. She hated picking the okra because it was all itchy and prickly but knew she couldn't just let it rot on the vine.

They ate tomatoes and cucumbers with lots of salt for their lunch. There were so many vegetables left over she felt bad about having to throw any of them away. Gran always said there were children starving all around the globe so no food should go to waste.

Glad you remembered that valuable lesson, Abbey. Don't throw this lovely food away, share it.

"Thank you for that reminder, Gran," Abbey said out loud.

"Is Gran talking to you again, Abbey?" Levi asked. He looked up to the ceiling and all around the room, then raised his voice and said, "Hi, Gran. I bet you don't recognize me anymore. I was just a little baby when you... left us. I'm all big now."

"She isn't floating on the ceiling and she isn't deaf. Gran remembers you and she loves you, Levi. She still has prayers for you floating around the universe," Abbey told him. "And she wants me to share this food but I'm not sure how. We can't get all the way across town to share with Mrs. Jarvis. And we can't get to church."

"We can share with our neighbors!" Levi said. "I bet Miss Yvonne and her little kids would love to have fresh vegetables."

Abbey answered, "Good idea, Levi. We just have to figure out how. We can't go inside anybody's house and we can't skip over anybody. There's six families on our street. Let's go check out those old baskets in the garden shed. I know there are a few peck baskets. Even if we divide this stuff by five, we can probably fill up the baskets."

They were able to scrounge up ten old peach baskets. Five were pint-sized and five were peck-sized. They loaded up five peck-baskets with tomatoes, a few cucumbers, some asparagus, and lots of okra. Fried okra was one of Levi's favorite dishes, so Abbey planned to make that for him for supper that night.

They wrote a note to put in every basket:

FROM OUR GARDEN TO YOU. ENJOY! YOUR NEIGHBORS, ROSE, ABBEY, AND LEVI WHIT @ 823

They decided it best to add Mom's name on the note and also to include their house number so the people who'd never met them would know where the stuff came from. Abbey decided to add a ribbon to the handle on each of the baskets. Her great-great grandmother's story about how important ribbons were lingered in her mind. *This is for you, Grandma Virginia. I wish I'd known you.*

When everything was ready to go, Abbey started having second thoughts. She was afraid maybe the neighbors would think it was dumb and would scoff at her and her brother. Levi, on the other hand, was a tornado of energy and excitement. He couldn't wait to share their bounty with everybody. He asked Abbey if they could take a picture of the baskets to show Mom when they talked to her that night.

They deposited the baskets on each of their neighbors' front porches and rang the doorbell, then raced back to the street so they wouldn't risk spreading their germs by being in close contact with anybody. Only three of their neighbors answered their doors. Those people hollered "Thank You!" and waved at the children. One of their neighbors was a very old man who God-blessed them for the food.

Miss Yvonne and her children all came to the door. The girls squealed with delight at the basket. Yvonne told them she had been longing for fresh vegetables and had only been serving up canned goods because they were easier to have delivered to their house. She asked Abbey and Levi to wait just a minute before they moved on. Then, she brought out a plate of cupcakes she said she'd just made that morning. "I hope you like strawberry cake," she said. "These are the girls' favorite. You can bring the plate back any time and just leave it here on the steps."

"We love strawberry cake!" Levi assured her.

They had a foot race back home. Abbey slowed down at the end and let Levi win. If he ever got that growth spurt their mom kept talking about, she knew he'd actually beat her one day. For now, she was OK with just letting him think he'd won.

She told Levi they could have one cupcake each and save the other two for after supper. She thought she might call Davey and tell him he could come by their back porch and get some tomatoes and her extra cupcake later. She knew there wasn't much food at his house, probably not ever anything homemade. She was still mad at him but as long as he didn't come inside, she knew Mom would be OK with her sharing food with him. Mama never turned away anybody who was hungry and tomato sandwiches were about the best summer food ever and there was no cooking involved. Perfect for Davey whom she knew couldn't boil water.

After they ate lunch, Abbey decided to read more of her grandma's journal. She left Levi in his room with his dictionaries and the *Lincoln Library* and went back to her mom's room to pick up where she'd left off in her grandma's journal.

Dear Journal. October 3, 1918. Sorry I haven't been keeping up writing. There's always so much to do and Mama's Headaches are getting worse so I have to help out with the little ones a lot. School's been off and on all year on account of the grippe, as some calls it, or the Spanish flu, as the doctors call it. Once somebody in class gets it, they shut school down for two weeks.

Today is my birthday. I'm about all grown up now, 11 years old. They're having another go at letting us kids go to school again but we have to wear a piece of cloth over our mouth and nose to keep the flu germs off-a us. Makes no difference to me though. Mama is abed most of the time and papa's out working in the fields and somebody has to take care of baby Rose, Cat, and Richard. So, I get up at dark and fix papa an egg (I hate going out to the chicken coop to get eggs when it's dark outside, I'm always afraid a snake will grab my hand when I reach in to pluck out the eggs), and wrap up a cold biscuit and a piece of bacon if there is any and put it in the old tin pail he totes with him to the cotton fields for his dinner break.

Mama was able to stir around a little today so she told me I could go to school and she'd watch out for the little ones. I was so happy! This was going to be a good birthday after all! My mama was going to get better and I was going to be free to go to school.

But papa saw me walking by and stopped me and asked me where I thought I was a-going. I told him mama was up and about and had sent me to school. He said, I'm awful sorry, Gin (that's what papa calls me) ain't no way you're going to school no more, big as you are. Your mama and me depend on you to help us out. Families have to stick together in hard times and help each other.

He asked me how old I was and I told him. He thought I was older on account of how tall I am. Mama is little like her people but I am big like papa and his people. Papa flung a burlap sack to me and told me to start filling it up. I was ashamed to be crying but I couldn't help it. Papa didn't notice though, he'd already turned away and walked down the row where he'd dropped his sack and picked it up again.

The thing about picking cotton is this: the bolls are so hard to pull and they're awful prickly, they make your fingers bleed something fierce. Also, the more you pick, the tired-er you get and the heavier the sack gets so the more you pick the more you think your back will break clean in half. By dinner time I was all wore out. I had a boiled egg wrapped up for my own dinner break but I was too dog-tired to eat it. I laid down in between the rows of cotton and fell asleep.

It was almost dark when I woke up. I feared papa would be sore mad at me for laying down on the job but he wasn't. He just told me I'd get better at picking cotton the more I did it. I handed him my sack, it was a pitiful effort I know. Not even half full. He told me don't worry you done your best. Seeing how tired I was, he kindly picked me up and carried me in his arms all the way home. Like I was light as a feather. I will never forget how big and strong my papa is.

When we got back to the house and mama saw me she screamed out. I looked down at myself and noticed that both my Hands was cut up and blood had run down both the sleeves on my dress and I looked a fright. Mama thought my hands had been chopped off I was so bloody. She fussed at papa for making me pick cotton and told him she wouldn't hear of that happening ever again. Papa told her she wasn't no rich princess any more and everybody had to pull their own weight around here. She told him to Shut Up! And, I am the mother of these children, I'll be the one who decides what activities they partake in. What were you thinking, making this child work like a field hand? That's the only time I ever heard my mama raise her voice like white trash and yell at anybody.

I feared I'd maybe get a whooping from papa for ruining my school dress. I only had the one and now I'd gone and messed it up by bleeding all over it. Mama would have to soak it and scrub it and who knows if she *could ever get all the blood out of that poor dress. It was a mite too tight and short for me, my legs just wouldn't stop growing, and it itched me something fierce, but a new dress for school was out of the question. There'd be no new frocks for me until Christmas, as usual.*

But papa didn't give me any mean eyebrows, nor tell me to go cut a hickory switch so he could whoop me with it. He went out to the well in the yard to wash his face and hands. And mama turned straight to the pump in the kitchen and pumped water in the dish pan, then poured some hot water from out of the iron kettle on the stove in with it to warm it up. Then she got out her bottle of rose water that she saved for special occasions and poured a little of that in the pan.

She pulled my school dress off of me and left me in my drawers while she soaked my hands in the scented water. I saw tears running down her face while she bathed my hands. I told her not to cry that it didn't hurt so very bad.

She bathed me all over in that warm water like I was a little baby but I didn't care. I love my mama so much I can't even explain it and I wanted to be her baby even if I was half grown. She put my nightgown on me and showed me where she had mended the hole in the front by embroidering a rose over where the hole had been. A real true to life Birthday present for me! She only had yellow thread, so the rose was yellow. I believe yellow roses are the most beautiful flowers God ever made and my mama is the most beautiful and smart and kind mama God ever made.

So, my birthday ended on a good Note after all. I love my new embroidered gown so much I asked mama if I could wear it under my dress to church. She laughed at me in the way she always does. With her eyes staying sad.

Dear Journal. October 4, 1918. Today, my mama went out to the fields to pick cotton beside papa.

Abbey's heart ached for the little girl her great-great grandmother had been. She felt ashamed of herself for complaining about not having a cell phone and complaining that she had to go to middle school. She hoped she could remember to be thankful for the things she and Levi had.

After supper she made her usual call to Miss Robin to check on their mom. Mom was looking stronger every day now. She listened to Levi's excited retelling of the day's events. He held up the picture of the baskets with vegetables in them he'd printed out that afternoon and told her about Miss Yvonne giving them homemade strawberry cupcakes.

When Mom asked who was taking care of them Abbey started to tell her Mrs. Jarvis would gladly … but her mom started coughing again and Miss Robin told them Mom needed to rest. Abbey felt so bad about leaving the sentence about Mrs. Jarvis unfinished but she knew her mom would worry herself to death if she knew they were all alone. And, she would think Abbey was truly crazy if she told her mom that Gran was there in the house with them, guiding them.

I usually advise that honesty is the best policy, Abbey, but in this case, perhaps something just short of the whole truth might be prudent, Gran whispered to her.

Abbey agreed with her grandmother on that point.

Chapter 16: *Posterior (adjective)*, Of or Near the Rear or Back Part

Dear Journal. October 20, 1918. We're having a cold snap which I hope will not last, but it probably will. The sheriff is allowing churches to be open but he warns he will shut them down again if parishioners start getting sick with the Flu which is killing people all over the world and has made it over here to us in the mountains. I hear tell that even our strong and brave soldiers who are busy fighting around the globe in The Great War are dying of this horrible influenza just the same as they are dying of bullets.

I got to wear my newly embroidered nightgown to church after all. Mama has let my winter coat out twice already but I've grown so much I still can't get it buttoned up so I had to wear my nightgown underneath my dress so's I'd have another layer to keep me warm.

But, me and my nightgown were not the most interesting thing about church today.

Usually, our church that we go to is uninteresting to the point of being boring. I feel bad for the Lord and all His angels who has to stick around here waiting to see who will answer the call and go down to the altar to repent (so They can be there for any of us poor souls who needs them). Just like us, They have to wait for Preacher Gibson to wrap it up which means they have to listen to him as he drones on and on. Dry as a bone. God must surely have the patience of Job.

I like our Bible study time at home better because my mama's a good reader, when she reads passages to us kids we feel like we're really there in the Holy Lands. And my papa's a card! He acts out a lot of the stories and makes us all howl and laugh. Mama says its ok to laugh when we study and think on the Lord for we are taught to "enter into His courts with joy."

Today is Homecoming at church. Our service started off dry as usual and I sat warm and cozy next to my mama, wearing my beloved nightgown under my Sunday dress. Allowing my mind to wander as it usually does when Preacher Gibson gets going. Today, instead of starting right in, Preacher called for testimonies. Good, thought I, testimonies always liven things up considerable. Brother Dellinger stood and told how God had healed his daughter of the polio. It was truly a miracle and before you know it, people were shouting and praising the Lord for all they were worth. I was truly thankful myself. I have a great fear of polio and do thank God for sending healing to my friend Pearl Dellinger.

Next thing you know, Brother Benton and his wife both got caught up in the Spirit. Brother Benton is a tall, skinny man, over six-foot. He got so excited he jumped the pew in front of him and went running up to the altar. His wife, Sister Carol, God bless her, is a little, short woman who's about as big around as she is tall. She was feeling the Spirit move her as well, so she tried to follow her husband over the pew. Since her legs were so short, she tripped up, and wound up falling flat on her face, passed out on the altar. Problem was, when she took a spill, her dress tail flew up over her head, leaving her behind parts out in clear view. Worse still, for some unknown reason, Sister Carol wasn't wearing no under drawers.

All of a sudden, the shouting and praising stopped and you could have heard a pin drop, the sanctuary got as quiet as a tomb. Then, the children started giggling and laughing. I knew better for I did not want to be pinched by my mama for making noise in church. I locked my eyes down to my lap where the Bible lay open to the 23rd Psalm. I moved my lips as if I was trying to memorize the verses but I know that didn't fool my mama. I'd memorized that Psalm years ago.

Brother Benton tried to sit his wife up but she out-weighed him by a good bit and he couldn't get a firm handle on her. She was dead weight. He never thought to cover her, (modesty not being a top priority of the male persuasion), he just kept trying to sit her up and she kept sliding back down in a faint. Every slide wrenched her dress up closer and closer to her chin. Preacher Gibson and a few of the deacons finally broke out of their embarrassed freeze and went to help Brother Benton but they couldn't quite figure out where to grab a-hold. They stood in a circle around her, with their hands in their pockets, looking down at her in her full glory.

Mama got her fierce look on her face. She handed baby Rose to me, got up and marched to the altar. She shooed the men away. Then, she took her shawl off and laid it over Sister Carol's lower forty. A few more ladies joined her, all adding their own shawl or coat to mama's. Mama took Sister Carol's head and held it in her lap. One of the ladies rushed off to get a glass of water. Another used her church fan and fanned Sister's face which was flushed.

My mama was the Hero of the day! Preacher announced if all hearts and minds are clear, we will close out this service and move on to the picnic stage of the day's events. The congregation sent up a loud and unanimous AMEN! Preacher had the men go on outside to set up the trestle tables under the trees. The ladies who weren't nursing Sister Carol back to consciousness set about laying out all the food on the tables.

Boy! Can the ladies of our church cook! We all ate until we were stuffed. Like the Lord tells us to do, we fellowshipped with one another in a spirit of love. I love my church and my neighbors. Mostly. I continue to pray to God to remove any hard feelings I may have toward some people. I will refrain from naming any names at this time.

P.S. To my knowledge, nobody told Sister Carol about her "dress accident," I hope nobody ever does for she would be mortified and also would probably feel the need to move on down the road to another church and I would miss her. She is the only lady in our congregation who ever comes by and checks in on mama when she's feeling poorly so I love her for that.

Chapter 17: *Nascent (adjective)*, First Stage of a Developmental Process; Beginnings

Abbey waited until Levi went to bed to call Davey. She decided to text rather than call anyway. She wasn't sure how mad she'd still be if she heard his voice. No matter how mad he made her, he also had the infuriating ability to make her forget how mad she was and then make her laugh. She was determined to stand firm on her decision not to allow him to come inside anymore while Mom was in the hospital. But, she and Levi both missed him and she wanted to share their food with him.

She finished the text to Davey, telling him she had food for him and please come by and pick it up. She told him she'd leave it outside on the porch steps and he could come any time to get it. She added that he couldn't come inside until Mom got home but she'd love to talk to him tomorrow and she was sorry for being grumpy with him. She placed the basket with tomatoes and the strawberry cupcake on the back porch step.

Davey walked out of the darkness and spoke, "Hey."

Startled, Abbey jumped and said, "How did you get here so fast? Are you stalking us or something?"

He said, "Nope. Not stalking. I was on my way over to leave a note for you. Guess I'll just hand it to you."

Abbey took the folded paper from him. Instead of reading it, she stuck it in her pocket and said, "What is this? Why were you going to leave me a note?"

"Time for me to be moving on. I didn't want to go without saying goodbye."

"What? Going where? What's going on Davey? You can't leave us now. We need you!"

He set his backpack down on the bottom step and said, "I'm sorry, Abbey. I know things are tough for you right now but I can't stay any more. Your mom will be back soon and you and Levi will both be fine. You don't need me. Not really."

"How can you say that? You know that isn't true." Abbey felt shame at begging but she couldn't help it. She felt as if she were losing a lifeline.

"I have to get out now, while I still can. You have no idea how bad things are with my dad. He hasn't been sober in weeks. He lost his job. He blames me for everything. I can't take it any more."

Abbey stuttered over her words. "But, but, I don't understand. Your leaving won't make him any less drunk, will it? He'll still be a wreck. Don't you think he needs you to help keep him stable?"

"I've taken care of him all of my life, Abbey. I can't do it any more. I'm not as good a person as you are. I'm all packed up and heading out. I figured I'd walk down to the underpass tonight. I've slept there before. Then it's not so far to the trucking terminal where my dad works. Used to work. I'll set out for there in the morning."

"Are you saying all this to get back at me for yelling at you for taking Mom's car? I told you I'm sorry I yelled at you."

"This has nothing to do with you, Abbey. You never stay mad for very long anyway. It's just time for me to go," Davey said.

"What about your dad? Is he moving somewhere too? Is he OK with this?" she asked.

"Just me. Dad's passed out. As usual. I'm not telling him that I'm leaving. He'll figure it out in a few days when he runs out of cigarettes or beer and I'm not there to do a store run for him."

"That's crazy talk, Davey. Please, let's hash this out. If we both use our heads, we can figure something out." She handed him the cupcake from the basket and told him to sit on the step beside her to eat it. He hesitated before sheepishly moving to sit beside her. That's when she saw his face in the circle of light thrown out by the back porch light. His right eye was swollen shut. He had scratches and bruises on his arms and little round dark circles all over every place she could see.

"What happened to you? Did you wreck on your skateboard?"

"You've obviously never been beat down by somebody bigger than you. Or been used as an ashtray by an old drunk who thinks you're too big for your britches," Davey said.

Abbey reached out to touch his face but he winced and pulled away. "Don't do that, Abbey. And don't feel sorry for me. That makes everything worse. I don't want you to ever feel sorry for me. Anything but pity. Not from you."

"Please tell me what happened. Friends share their problems, remember?" Abbey said.

"Same old. Same old," Davey said. "He was drunk and mad and he took it out on me. Like always. This time I gave him some lip, said I wasn't going to take his crap any more. So, he showed me who was boss. He's right. I'm not strong enough to stand up to him. And I can't take being his punching bag any more. So, I'm leaving."

"Take the time to think this through, Davey. You can't run away from home," Abbey said. "Where would you even go? You said you didn't know where your mom is."

"Dad has people up outside Raleigh somewhere. Couple a years ago his step-brother came down here and said he was looking for help at this body shop he'd just opened. Offered dad a job. I thought I'd look him up and see if he's still looking to hire somebody."

"You're fourteen years old. You can't get a job. And what about school? You have to stay in school until you're at least sixteen. Did you forget about that?" Abbey said.

"I'll be fifteen in less than two months. You can get a work permit when you're fifteen. But Uncle Larry's place isn't exactly above-board. He pays under the table. That's no problem."

"What about school? You plan on dropping out? Do you know what that means for your future? And, even if you're dumb enough to drop out, you can't do that till you're sixteen. They'll put your dad in jail if he doesn't send you to school."

Davey shook his head and smiled. "My future? I'm not even enrolled in school this year. Do you know how many days I went to school last year? About thirty. And that's being generous. The vice-principal came out to talk to dad and dad met him at the door with a shotgun and told him to turn right back around and mind his own business. Dad told him we were homeschooling, thank you for your concern."

"And, the principal believed that?" Abbey was incredulous. She'd never met Davey's father but if anybody answered the door with a shotgun and then threatened to shoot the principal, she didn't think she'd believe that person was big on academics.

"Maybe he did. Maybe he thought it'd be better for his health if he just wrote me off. Abbey people like me... we, we don't count. We're invisible. Nobody knows if we're in school. Nobody knows if we aren't. Maybe people like me matter in movies. But not in real life. We make the school's numbers look bad if we're out too much or if we just don't show up. So, they write us up as 'transferred' and forget about us."

"I care about you. I care what happens to you. Mom and Levi and I all care, Davey. You are important. To us. To me." Abbey tried not to cry because she knew Davey would think she felt sorry for him, which she did. She wished she could make him see how valuable his life was.

She wished she could take him to the place where prayers and tears and wishes make everybody stronger.

The goodness and love of God surrounds all of us, Abbey, her gran said. *It never wanes. Davey can find comfort there, he only has to open his heart and reach out and accept it. He is a child of God just like you and Levi. Don't give up on him.*

"I won't," Abbey said out loud. "I won't give up on you, Davey. I believe in you. I will *never* stop believing. Or caring." She brushed her tears away and continued, "If I can't talk you out of going, let me help you make a plan. Like you helped me and Levi." Abbey thought if Davey took the time to actually lay out a plan he'd see the futility of running away. "How do you plan to get all the way to Raleigh? And how will you find your uncle when you get there?"

"One a-my dad's buddies drives a day route to Raleigh and back every day. He'll give me a ride. I'll be down at the terminal early and catch him before he leaves. I already looked up the body shop. It's still in business. Since I can't work legal, that means I work cheap. He'll hire me on. No problem. I'll wait and call Uncle Larry after I get to Raleigh. I don't want him trying to call my dad before I can make it out of town."

"You don't think your uncle will call your dad when you get there and have him come and pick you up?" Abbey asked.

"My dad's not exactly the go-out-of-your-way for anything or anybody kind of guy. He'd stop me if I was conveniently passing by the couch but no way is he driving to Raleigh to bring me back. That's even more out of his way than driving himself down to the Quiky Mart for beer."

"If you change your mind…" Abbey said. She was all out of arguments that could make him want to stay.

"You'll be the first to know. Tell Levi 'bye for me. And your mom. I know she'll be all cured and home before you know it. Thanks for the cupcake. And the tomatoes. I bet Uncle Larry likes tomato sandwiches. Butter him up a little." Davey picked up his backpack and the basket of tomatoes, gave her a little salute, turned and walked away.

"Davey, wait," Abbey said. She ran down the steps and hugged him. "Please call me and let me know how you're doing. OK? And, try to believe, Davey. God is there waiting to help you. You just have to believe."

"You bet," he said.

Then he was gone.

After a time, Abbey went back inside. She locked up the house then looked in on Levi. She forgot about the note until it fell out of her pocket when she took off her shorts to put her pajamas on.

She felt old and tired and sad. She wondered how anybody could live with this much hurt inside of them. She wished she had Levi's gift with words. Maybe she could have persuaded Davey to stay.

Do you believe you have the right to ask him to change his life for you? Gran said.

"I don't know, Gran. His dad is awful. And he isn't going to school anyway. He doesn't think anybody cares about him. Maybe he's right about school and his dad. He's never had a chance. His whole life has been crappy. It just isn't fair."

Life so rarely is, Gran answered.

Abbey unfolded the note.

Dear Abey, I'm so glad I met you. Your the best friend I ever had. You're the prettiest and smartest girl in the whole world. I will never love anybody else like I love you. Thank you for everything you taught me about how some people can be good and kind. I never knew that before. Your friend forever, Davey.

Chapter 18: *Lugubrious* (*adjective*), Full of Sorrow

Abbey didn't want to upset Levi any more than she absolutely had to so she told him they probably wouldn't be seeing Davey around for a while because he was going to visit with his uncle in Raleigh.

Perceptive as always, Levi said, "We're so lucky we have the family we have. Poor Davey's not got anybody to look after him like we do. Even our dead grandma looks out for us. Poor Davey."

"Yeah, well, I'd keep the 'dead grandma' thing to myself if I were you. We don't want the looney tunes squad coming to lock us away," Abbey told him.

After watching their church online and eating lunch, Abbey and Levi each went their separate ways. Oh, the glory of having a house with a bedroom for each of them! Abbey picked up her great grandma's journal and settled in on her mom's bed with a cozy comforter, plumped up pillows, and settled in to read.

Dear Journal. November 24, 1918. Today is beautiful baby Rose's third-month birthday. Also, it is her last.

About two weeks after Homecoming, I came down with a cough and fever. Then followed Mama, Rose, Cat, and Richard. Papa was the only one spared of the grippe. Which is what papa kept telling us was what we had but mama and I both knew it was the world-wide flu that had taken a hold of us. Poor, precious, beautiful Rose. How could a weak, tiny baby hope to survive such a thing when it felled strong men armed with rifles, fighting out in the trenches?

Richard and Cat have got so skinny I can almost see right through them. They've hacked and coughed so hard they've wore themselves out and often faint away. Mama and the baby grew so weak they couldn't cough at all. They were most often still as the grave, slick with sweat, and hardly breathing.

There is no use in me or anybody else running for help. There will be no help coming for us. The Sheriff came out and painted a big black X on our front door to let everybody who happened to pass by know there was contagion in our house and Do Not Enter. Thankfully, I snapped out of my sickness pretty quick and set about doing my best to help papa take care of the ones who are still sick. Papa slaughtered a pullet and had me pluck it and clean it and make chicken soup to feed our patients. This remedy has helped Cat and Richard considerable.

Mama has been able to sit up for about a week. Last night baby Rose stopped whimpering and got quiet and still. Around her nose and mouth she had turned blue. Mama bathed her and wrapped her in our softest blanket, which was a present to mama from Miss Eugenie. Papa told mama to be realistic and use an old blanket to wrap the baby in, but mama beat him with her fists and said, "Do not tell me how to take care of my baby. Her skin is too tender to use a rough blanket on, she needs to be swaddled in this soft one. I won't have her getting cold."

Mama rocked Rose for most of the day today and sang a lullaby to her even though she knows Rose is gone. Papa tried twice to take the baby from mama but he got smacked at and finally gave up.

Around suppertime, he told me to keep a good eye on everything and he'd be right back, he had an errand he had to run. Less than an hour later he returned with Sister Carol, whose husband had died about a week ago of the very same condition, that horrible flu that the devil sent over to us all *the way from Spain. She said she wasn't afraid to come around us because she had nursed Brother Benton and never caught the flu herself.*

She gave me a hug and apologized for not coming sooner. She knew we'd been declared off-limits because the sheriff kept the list of diseased households updated and posted outside-a the post office. The sheriff had also posted one of his deputies outside the post office. The deputy on guard duty only allows people to come in one at a time. When you call for your mail, you have to stand way over by the front door, pull your mask down real quick so Mr. Howard, the Postmaster, can see who you are. Then, Mr. Howard goes in back, gets your mail and puts it out on the ledge in front of his call window. Then he shuts the window so as not to pick up any-a your germs whist you come forward and pick up your mail.

Sister Carol said she knew it was her Christian duty to come and see about us young'uns but she was so wrought with sorrow about losing her husband it took her a few days to pull herself together. She said she'd prayed and prayed for all -a us and I believe her. I know she cares for us and she loves my mama.

She went into mama and papa's bedroom where mama still sat in her rocker, singing to the baby and holding her close. She stayed in there with mama for over an hour and when she came out, she was carrying little Rose in her arms. The baby looked like she was only sleeping. I don't believe I'll ever see another baby as perfect as Rose is. I asked Sister Carol to let me hold my sister and she did.

Papa came inside wiping dirt from his hands. He motioned for Sister Carol and me to follow him back outside. He had dug a small grave in between mama's beloved yellow rose bushes which are dormant now in the winter but will be bursting with blooms when spring rolls back around.

Papa took Rose from me and held her in his arms and kissed her face. Then, he wrapped her up good and tight and laid her gently in the hole in the earth. When he shoveled dirt to cover her up, I had to look away, I just couldn't stand to watch that. Part of my heart got buried too and I know it will forever stay right here in our side yard, under mama's rose bushes.

Sister Carol has a beautiful singing voice. She sang "In the Sweet By and By, we shall meet on that beautiful shore." Even if

I had a fine singing voice, I couldn't have joined in, all I could do was cry. Papa asked me to recite some scripture. I didn't trust my voice but more than anything I didn't want to let my papa down. Hadn't he already done the most difficult task any person could imagine – dig a grave for your own baby?

The passage that came to my mind was the 23rd Psalm, which mama recites to us children most every night. When I got to the Yea, though I walk through the valley of the shadow of death, part, I couldn't say it. My voice just wouldn't keep talking. Sister Carol finished reciting the Psalm for me and Papa said, "Amen."

She put her arm around my shoulders and walked me back toward the house. I asked Papa if he wasn't coming in with us and he said, "No, I've got some things to do out here." He asked Sister Carol if she would kindly stay with mama and the kids for the night and he'd take her home in the morning. He said he'd sleep outside under the shed tonight.

I could hear Papa choking and retching outside. I went to open the door and go check on him, deeply afeared he had taken sick too. Sister Carol stayed my hand before I could pull the door open and told me to let Papa be. She said he needed to grieve in private. I said but I don't want him to be alone. She told me he isn't alone, he's with his baby girl and his God.

Papa is the biggest, strongest man I know. He has never cried, even when he 'bout cut his whole leg clean off splitting wood. The sound of my papa sobbing and crying out to God is the most mournful thing I've ever heard.

How can any heart hurt so bad and still keep on beating?

Chapter 19: *Calamitous* (adjective), Tragically Devastating

Dear Journal. December 20, 1918. I haven't had ~~no~~ any time to write down my thoughts. It's almost Christmas in the year of our Lord Jesus Christ 1918. All I wanted for Christmas was for mama to get better and my papa to find work that pays. None of that happened. Last week my mama went off to town looking for a doctor to treat her terrible headaches. She only made it as far as the railroad crossing. Which is where the sheriff told papa they found her body. She must of fell down and couldn't get out of the way in time. The conductor said he was surely sorry but he hadn't had time to stop before he hit my mama.

We can't afford a marker for her grave so I'm full of fear that she will pass from this world with no notice from nobody. We laid her to rest beside Rose, in the shade of mama's beautiful rose bushes. My mama's name is Janey Rose and she is the most beautiful woman in the world and has long beautiful brown hair that she lets me help her comb through sometimes at night. I want the whole world to know that she lived and was loved by us. I wish my heart could be mended like mama mended my nightgown but there ain't no pretty yellow rose ever going to be stitched over this big hole in my heart.

Preacher came out to say words over mama, unlike with baby Rose. He and his wife had both suffered with the Spanish flu and recovered so he didn't fear being around us this time. He told me my mama was happy and at rest but I don't think I believe him even though he knows the scriptures by heart. I think my mama's sad because of she needs me as much as I need her so both of us is sad because we are apart.

Sister Edith told me to hush up crying and be a big girl and help my papa. I don't like her a-tall. She's the loudest Amen-er in church and also the most sour person I ever knew, her mouth always turns down and she sniffs like somebody left the outhouse door open. She brought over pinto beans and cornbread and an apple pie for us all though and I served it right up. No matter how mean you are, if you go to the trouble of *making food for us, we will most surely partake of it.*

Sister Edith is a widow-woman and she keeps giving papa the eye. He is a big, strong, and handsome man. I think she's set her cap for him. I sure hope he don't fall for that.

He's leaving at first light in the morning to go to somewhere around the middle of the state where people say they are hiring strong men to work in the textile mills and also day laborers. The men who owns the mills must be rich as kings. For months now they've been sending big, open bed trucks through town, rounding up men. They yell out to all: "Listen up fellers! Come with us if you want to make good money! There's work for all that wants it! Climb on board and go with us to the land of milk and honey!"

Papa always said he didn't want nothing to do with any city work but since he can't make a living share-cropping here he can't be choosey. As mama always says, Beggars Can't Be Choosers. So, like most of the other men around here, he's going to turn his back on mountain life and climb up on that truck and go off to find riches in the land of the cotton mills.

Dear Journal. January. (I don't know the exact date, lost track of time sorry). Christmas came and went and now it's 1919. Papa's still gone. He left me a cord of wood so I could keep the fire going while he was gone but it's so wet and cold I can't keep anything warm or dry. Richard only has three diapers and he's always wet. The whole cabin smells like pee all the time on account of he wets the bed including me and Cat and I can't get anything washed and dried in time to change him again. His bottom is red as fire. I don't have any powder or grease to put on it. I'm just letting him run bare-bottom today. I sure hope papa gets home soon. I'd even take kindly to mean old Sister Edith coming over if she'd give me a hand with these two.

Dear Journal. February 14, 1919. Well, a lot has changed in this past year since I first got this journal. Every time I write in it I think of mama and cry for the love of her and for how sorely I miss her. I will forever be the girl who hasn't got a mama.

Abbey drifted off to sleep and dreamed she was back in their tiny apartment and mama was at work and Levi was crying and she was so tired she couldn't hold her eyes open.

"Abbey. Abbey! Wake up, it's almost seven-forty-five. You fell asleep. It's time to call Mom." Levi was standing at the bedside shaking her to get her awake.

"What? seven-forty-five already? Man! I must be really tired." She told Levi to turn the light on while she called their mom.

Miss Robin wasn't at work. Somebody else answered her phone. Turns out it was a hospital phone. The man filling in for Miss Robin told Abbey her mom had had a bad day and wouldn't be able to talk to them tonight.

"What does that mean? A bad day? Is she worse? What's happening to her?" Abbey said.

"It just means she's not feeling so good right now. Try to stay calm. She needs for you and your brother to be calm, so she won't have to worry about you. We don't want her worrying about anything but getting better, do we?"

"No, *we* don't want her worrying at all. *We* want her back home." Abbey's voice cracked but she struggled to stay in control of her emotions. She didn't like this man. He talked down to her like she was stupid. Miss Robin never did that. "Can I call back in an hour or so and check in on her?"

"I think not. Everything's crazy around here tonight. We're slammed. And short-staffed. None of that your problem, sorry."

Abbey could hear sirens and bells going off in the background. People were shouting.

"Gotta go. I'll give you a call back later tonight if I can. Can't promise anything though," and he hung up.

Levi looked all pitiful, his bottom lip quivering. He started to talk but she shushed him.

"Don't you start, Levi. Don't you dare. We'll call back before we go to bed. Until then, not a word from you. Let's go eat supper and watch a movie. I'll let you pick which one."

"But, but he said we couldn't call back," Levi stammered.

"What did I say? Not a word. Go pick out a movie. I'll heat up supper."

"Can we watch SpongeBob again?"

Abbey rolled her eyes. She had no one to blame but herself. What did she expect he'd pick?

It could be so much worse, Gran whispered in her ear.

Don't I know it, Abbey thought back. Then, she added, *Dear God, please don't let me and Levi be the children who don't have a mama.*

Chapter 20: *Camaraderie (noun)*, Friendship

Dear Journal. July 15, 1919. Papa moved us out of the mountains down to the middle of the state where everything's flat as a flitter. Even though he hates doing City work, he's found him a place in the cotton mill where he is soon to be promoted to lead-man if all goes as planned. His boss man promised there'd be a job for me there soon but I hope that never pans out.

Papa's married him a new wife name of Annie Mae. I like her all right and am happy about how mad Sister Edith was when he brought Annie Mae home with him. Annie Mae asked me to call her mama but I never will. Janey is my mama forever. No offense intended toward Annie Mae. My mama's passing is in no wise Annie Mae's fault.

I got to go to school for a few weeks but now it's summer so school's out. I wish I could go to school all the time and learn everything there is to learn. Geography is my favorite subject. The world is surely a big place and I hope to see lots of it one fine day. I wonder what it was like for Dr. Livingstone's children to go explore deepest, darkest Africa with their papa. I feel like they were very lucky children. But I know I mustn't envy them because envy is a deadly sin.

Dear Journal. August 10, 1919. It's Sunday so I didn't have to go to work with papa today. The mills don't run on the Lord's Day. Annie Mae is sick and took to her bed so I can't go to church and have to watch after Cat and Richard, who is now out of diapers thankfully. Papa started taking me to work with him in the mill a few weeks ago. The foreman asked him how old I was on account of they are a progressive enterprise and have a strict rule about hiring female children under 12 years of age.

Boy children are deemed plenty old enough to work at a man's job by the time they are around 10 years old (unless they are sickly which is a great shame for their parents who are stuck with a child who isn't fitten to do much other than a job which doesn't require any physical labor).

But a-course how tall I am worked to my disadvantage, papa fudged a little on my *age for I won't be 12 until October but the foreman didn't ask me, he only asked papa and probably papa don't really know to the exact day how old I really am. He has bigger Fish to fry, like how's he supposed to feed us all?*

My day goes thusly, Annie Mae wakes me at five-fifteen before the rooster crows so I can use the outhouse, wash my face and hands, eat an egg, and be ready to walk to the mill with papa. The work whistle blows at six sharp and your pay will be docked if you are unlucky enough to be even one minute late. Or worse, you will get fired and there's ten more people in line behind you waiting for a job to open up, so you better be Johnny-On-The-Spot and never slow down if you want to keep this job. Which, I don't, if truth be told but I know my family depends on me, so I keep my thoughts to myself.

Most of us children work six days-per-week from six to six. Some of the kids are too short to reach the machines so they have to stand on a bench to reach the looms. Because of how tall I am I can reach but must stand on my tip toes often, which wears me out. When us kids get tired we help keep each other awake for if we fall asleep at our jobs the Boss Man will come by with a cane and give us licks and boy does that sting. I fell asleep one day and I can tell you I had welts on my legs and hindquarters for days.

Boss Man appears to truly enjoy catching us asleep for he really puts his back into the beatings and smiles the whole time he's doing it. I hate his evil grin. The Bible says if-n you harbor hate in your heart it's the same as murder. I know I would never put a knife to this man, but struggle as I may, I cannot rid myself of the hate he stirs in me. It's a good thing I don't own a knife because I'd hate to test my theory about never doing anybody bodily harm.

SPARE THE ROD AND SPOIL THE CHILD is written on a great big sign that hangs over our looms and you better believe our Boss has that verse memorized and is a true believer. I feel sorry for his own children and hope he doesn't beat them at home. I can't ask them because none of his own work here in the mill. I guess they're too rich to have to work.

Every Saturday is pay day. The Boss Man struts up and down the rows of machines, where us kids works, with a handful of little brown envelopes, each one containing our week's wages. He goes up to *each kid, shakes the envelope so we can hear the nickels jingling inside, and pretends like he's going to hand over the envelope with our name on it, then, if we are stupid enough to reach out for it, he snatches it away real quick and laughs at us.*

Everybody who's been here for more than one week knows we don't own the money we are paid and we are not allowed to even touch the pay envelopes. They go straight to our papas. One nickel a day for six days equals 30c per week for our work unless we got docked for falling asleep or coming in late. I feel like the worth of me and my life is measured out in little bitty, brown envelopes. I despise the sight of them.

On our way home on Saturdays, papa and I stop at the company store and buy food and goods for the next week. I get a special treat for being a good worker, which we don't mention to the kids at home. Papa buys a coke-a-cola and a pack of peanuts (one whole day's pay is the cost!) and we split it. We have us a seat on a bench outside the store, papa takes a swig then passes the coke-a-cola to me. I never tasted anything so delicious in my life! Papa pours the whole pack of peanuts in the coke-a-cola and they make it taste even more delicious. Sitting there beside papa, sharing a cold drink and salty peanuts, I forget about how sore my fingers are and how tired I am for a while.

One thing I don't forget is how bad I wish I was in school instead of in a cotton mill every day. And how much I miss my mama so I guess that's two things.

Abbey kept the journal on her nightstand and read a little bit most nights. Sometimes she couldn't read though because it made her so sad and she had trouble falling asleep. She hoped her prayers for her mom and Levi and Davey joined with the ones in Gran's "Mom Cave," and gave strength and energy and comfort to those she loved so dearly. Maybe God had another special place for holding on to children's prayers. Either way, she was pretty sure her prayers were pure energy too, just like the ones Gran showed her. And they'd live forever somewhere. God doesn't waste energy. Or love. He puts it all to good use.

Mom had good days and bad days. If she could get stable and stay that way, she would be able to come back home soon. Until that day, Abbey soldiered on to keep their home running smoothly as if Mom were still with them.

Levi and Abbey's gift of garden vegetables started a trend on their end of the neighborhood. Once or twice a week they got surprise gifts from people they were now coming to know as their friends, left, with notes, on their doorstep. Mr. and Mrs. Shaw from two doors down scored toilet paper from somewhere and left them four rolls! Mrs. Patel was an excellent knitter and made scarfs and gloves for both of them. Abbey hoped it would get cold this year so they could wear them.

They soon learned Miss Yvonne was a baker and caterer. Most Mondays she brought by samples of whatever dishes she had made for the previous weekend. Of course, the sweets were the children's favorite but they appreciated everything. Abbey didn't have to worry about cooking on those Mondays because they had Yvonne's delicious gifts to look forward to. When Covid was all over with, Miss Yvonne, who was a culinary college graduate, promised to give Abbey cooking lessons.

The Lowes, who lived next door, were a young couple with no children. Mr. Lowe started cutting their grass every week when he did his own yard. That was fabulous for Abbey who absolutely hated doing yard work. Abbey sent over warn brownies to thank him every time she made them because he liked them so much.

Much to Levi's delight, Mr. and Mrs. Hikara (Mr. Hikara, they came to learn, was the elderly man who had blessed them for the garden vegetables), started leaving books of word puzzles for him. One day Levi was playing in the front yard with the stray kitten who adopted him, when the Hikaras passed by on their daily evening walk. They stopped to chat with him (from a safe distance of course). When they found out Levi wanted to be a spelling bee champion, they told him about their daughter Lea who had been the state spelling bee champion when she was in middle school. Levi was star struck.

Leo, the stray kitten who was a tuxedo cat, very quickly became Leo, Levi and Abbey's cat. Levi brought him inside one night when a thunderstorm raged outside and blew tree branches across the road. No creature needed to be homeless out in that weather. Abbey felt a special sympathy for the kitten, who, like herself and her brother, found itself without a mother to care for it. Mr. Lowe, who asked them to call him Carl, was a veterinarian who took Leo into his office for a check-up and pronounced him healthy and flea-free, ready to be a good indoor cat. Also, he was a she, so Leo was rechristened Elsa.

Abbey tried to call or text Davey but his phone wasn't a working number any more. She couldn't find any place called "Larry's Body Shop," online, so she knew she'd just have to wait for Davey to contact her. She still prayed for him every night and hoped he was OK and maybe he'd be able to get his life straightened out and hopefully, get back in school. She hoped his Uncle Larry would be a better parent than Mr. Loftin had been. Her worry for him was compounded by her deep feelings for him. Sometimes she wished she'd never met him. If she didn't know him her heart could go back to being normal and hurt only for her mother. She vowed to never again give her heart to any boy. Who needs them, anyway?

Drew, Abbey's friend from middle school started texting. Since Abbey was now in possession of Mom's cell phone, she was free to text her friend without parental oversight. Not that she and Drew had things to say their mothers wouldn't approve of. The privacy was nice. It made them both feel grown up.

Drew said she loved her new house but hated having to do online classes and missed her old friends from back home. She couldn't express an opinion, one way or another, about her new town because since Covid had shut most everything down, the family hadn't been able to go out and explore. Likewise, she hadn't yet formed an opinion about her new school. How much can you judge a school if your only contact with it is via the internet?

Abbey didn't tell Drew about her and Levi being on their own with Mom in the hospital. She wasn't afraid Drew would narc them out; she just couldn't trust putting that information out into the universe. She still put her mom's name on all the gifts she and Levi left for the neighbors. So far, they had been able to carry on in peace and Abbey wanted it to stay that way.

Drew sometimes went on and on about clothes and shoes and not being able to go shopping in person any more. Abbey could not have cared less about clothes or shopping. She had so many other things to worry about. She sort of remembered what it was like to be excited about going shopping but those days were a lifetime away. Sometimes she felt like Drew was still a little girl who only thought about silly things. Abbey hoped she wasn't turning into a sour puss like Sister Edith. She thought this Covid had turned lots of people into crazy mean shut-ins. Of course, nobody could ever accuse Abbey of having a sunny disposition, but still, she wasn't morbid. She intended not to give in to the dire feeling of hopelessness as so many others had.

Drew told Abbey about her new crush, Anthony. She and Anthony waved to each other when they rode their bikes around the neighborhood. They hadn't had a close, in-person conversation yet, but Drew had been in love several times and she recognized love when she saw it. She knew that love from afar was still love. Although she'd never seen him without a mask, Drew firmly believed Anthony was the cutest boy she had ever met. Anthony's parents were both doctors and Anthony planned to follow in their footsteps and be a doctor when he grew up. Drew was already planning her wedding and how many children she'd have. She and Anthony talked on the phone every night after Drew's parents went to bed. She wasn't supposed to talk on the phone after lights out so she sat in her closet to talk to him, ensuring her parents couldn't hear.

Abbey liked listening to Drew's big plans and she was happy for her friend and thankful for her friendship. She wondered what her life would have been like if Mom hadn't gotten sick. She'd never have had to be in charge of Levi. Even if she continued doing most of the cooking, her mom would have been in charge of her and Levi and the house and their schoolwork. Her life could have been carefree like Drew's. Maybe she could have cultivated a relationship with Davey. She quashed that thought as soon as it reared its ugly head. Davey was not now and never had been her boyfriend. He considered her his friend, period. A friend who he'd turned his back on. She didn't blame him for leaving his awful home situation but she did blame him for not contacting her.

Knock on wood, so far, she and Levi were healthy and their mom's paycheck was still being deposited every other week so the bank draft that paid the utility bills was funded. Abbey wondered what Drew would think if she knew about Abbey having to worry about fixing meals and paying bills. Their great-great grandma Virginia may have had such things to worry about but Abbey didn't believe any of her own contemporaries could relate to her plight. In a lot of ways Abbey believed she had more in common with her great-great grandma than she did with her best friend.

When Drew asked Abbey if she had a boyfriend, Abbey hedged a bit and said she'd met a neighborhood boy who was nice but his family had moved away. Davey was alive and well in Abbey's heart and mind but she didn't entertain foolish thoughts of a big wedding and a slew of children. She hoped to meet up with Davey again one day but she was afraid to jinx it by saying it out loud, so she stayed mum.

She longed to talk to him. Their once daily conversations had sustained her for months. She wondered why he didn't miss them too. He had carved a huge hole in the center of her heart and losing him made her whole body ache. She felt ashamed of her foolishness in offering her heart to him. What an idiot she had been. She'd lowered her guard and allowed him to come in and now he was gone. And he had never felt anything for her other than casual friendship. Why would anyone ever love her? She was wholly unlovable. He probably left town to get away from her as much as from his dad.

Abbey made her nightly rounds: check the locks on the doors, load the dishwasher, wipe down the counter tops, straighten up their "school room," for the next day's work, get out her pajamas and run water for her bath, check in on Levi. *I am turning into my mother*, she thought.

Not a bad thing to turn into, Gran said back to her.

At 12-years-old? Give me a break, Gran. I should be doing girlie stuff not mommy stuff.

And just what kind of fun girlie stuff would you rather be doing? Gran wanted to know.

Before she could think of an honest reply, Mom's cell phone rang. The screen identified the caller as "Unknown." If it had been a "Scam Likely" Abbey wouldn't have answered. For some reason the "Unknown," scared her. She took the phone with her to the bathroom, turned off the water in the tub, and answered.

"Hello?" she said.

A man's voice said, "Rose? Is that you?"

Abbey's heart jumped into overdrive. She knew who the caller was. No way could she remember what his voice sounded like. Yet, somehow, she knew. She would not give him the satisfaction of knowing she knew who he was. He didn't deserve that. "Who is calling, please?"

He said, "Come on, it hasn't been that long. You aren't still mad about me coming by your work that time, are you? They messed up my account and I thought maybe you could straighten them out for me. You know, for old times' sake. Come on now, that's water under the bridge."

"What do you want?" Abbey asked.

"Can't a man just want to call and check in on his wife and kids? Boy, you must not think much 'a me if you're thinkin' I got some alterior motive or something."

Levi would have a conniption fit if he had heard "alterior."

"*Ex*-wife. What do you want, Sam?" Abbey said. She wanted to add, "and *abandoned* kids," but she didn't trust her voice wouldn't crack and she was determined not to let this jerk think she gave a hoot about him or his motives.

"I was just thinkin,' that's all. I might be passing through Trinity Hold in a day or so and I was thinkin' maybe I could stop by and look in on you. Or somethin'. No biggie. I was just thinkin' that's all."

Abbey cut off the call. She knelt by the tub and struggled to control her breathing. *This must be what Levi feels when he's having an asthma attack*, she thought.

Try to calm down, Abbey, Gran's voice said.

He thought I was Mom. He doesn't even know who I am or anything about me. And why do I even care? I don't care about him any more than he cares about me. I must really be losing it. Abbey fought to stem the tide of tears she just couldn't hold inside any longer. *I'm so tired, Gran. I'm tired of being in charge. I'm tired of being scared. I'm tired of worrying about Mom. I'm just tired. I want to be silly and superficial like Drew. I didn't ask for any of this responsibility.*

You have the police officer's card. Call him. Tell him you need help. He'll have somebody here by morning, maybe even tonight. You have options, Abbey. This is the course you chose for yourself, Gran whispered to her.

Yeah, right. I can call and have Child Protective Services come on over and 'protect' us by separating us and sending us who knows where and leaving our house without anybody to take care of it or make sure the bills get paid and when Mom gets home, she won't have a home to get back to. No thank you. This is my home. And Levi is my family and I'm taking care of him. I don't need anybody else. Except my mom. And you.

The bath water had gotten cold, so she turned on the hot water to warm it up. For added comfort, she poured some bubble bath liquid in. Then, she slipped into the warm water and soaked until her skin puckered and her nerves were soothed.

Nothing like a hot bubble bath to make everything right with the world, Gran said.

"I'm afraid things will fall apart, Gran. Levi and I have made it ok for so long now. I can't believe our luck will hold out. I just have a funny kind of feeling that something bad is going to happen."

Do you believe your life is ruled by luck? A roll of the dice determines your destiny? Gran asked.

"No, ma'am, I don't. Not exactly. But I have to be realistic. Something has been working in our favor for a long time. It can't last forever."

Oh, Abbey you have so much love poured out toward you. It's the tremendous power of that love that sustains you. That guides you. It isn't luck, honey. You are under the protection of all of us who love you, Gran said.

"Is my dad a bad man?" Abbey said.

A complex question, Gran said.

"I've been thinking about Davey and his dad. And Levi and me and our not-quite-dad. I think Davey's dad is truly a bad person. But I wonder if my dad is too. Davey's dad is cruel and abusive but my dad is just perpetually absent. Which one is worse?"

They're both bad. And equally harmful. Is it more hurtful, or sinful, to abuse your children, or to abandon them? Which is worse? Are there degrees of sin? Is stealing a million dollars more sinful than stealing a pack of chewing gum? Humans rank and prioritize sins sometimes. I'm not sure God does, Gran answered.

"Well, if you don't know, there's no way I can figure it out. I'm just a kid," Abbey said.

A leopard can't change his spots, Abbey. Your dad is who he is. He tried to be the man he needed to be, the man Rose and you and Levi needed for him to be. He couldn't sustain the pretense. It took too much effort. That effort was exhausting for him. It became more than he could bear. He was constantly struggling against his true nature. Until he gave up and went away.

"Are you saying people can't change? Dad can't grow up and accept responsibility, so it isn't his fault he dumped us. That's just who he is?"

That's not what I said, Abbey. And there's a big difference between 'can't' and 'won't'. At the core of our being, we are who we are. I think people like your dad have a missing gene or strand of DNA maybe. Whatever it is that gives us the ability to be selfless. To love unconditionally. You have it. Your mother and brother have it. Your dad doesn't. The only selfless love your dad feels is for himself.

"Did he ever love us?" Abbey asked.

I believe he did. In his own way. I believe he still does. And I think he has regrets about what a bad husband and father he was. I'm not sure he understands the depth of his neglect. I think he's gotten to be an expert at making up excuses for himself. But if he had the chance to do it again, he wouldn't change. He is who he is. I think it's so sad, he'll never know the joy of immersing himself in pure love.

"I hate him," Abbey said.

The opposite of love isn't hate. Love's opposite is something closer to apathy, I believe. Hate only hurts you, *Abbey. Try to get to a place where you can love him for who he is, the man who helped give you life. But accept the fact he won't be in your life like your mother is. Like she will always be. He can only hurt you if you give him the power to hurt you. Stop doing that.*

"Is that what I've been doing? Giving him power over me?"

She sat there a few minutes more, waiting for Gran to answer. When no answer came, she said, "OK, I'm going to bed now. Even if you won't tell me exactly what I want to know, I love you anyway. Please go hover over Mom or give her a hug or talk at her and scare the living crap out of her, whatever it is you do. Who knows how long it will be before we're allowed to visit her in the hospital. She's all alone there. I guess we're *all* alone for the time being."

Before she crawled under the covers, she noticed her bedroom window was open. *That's odd. I don't remember opening it today. I guess Dad's call really did rattle me.*

Before she could get the window closed, a strong breeze blew in and fluttered the pages of her Bible which was lying on her bedside table. The breeze suddenly dissipated, leaving the Bible open to Hebrews, chapter twelve: "Therefore, since we are surrounded by such a great cloud of witnesses, let us throw aside every weight that "burdens us."

Rest well, Little Abbey. You have never been alone. None of you have.

Chapter 21: *Feckless (adjective)*, Lacking Strength of Character

Abbey didn't tell Levi about the phone call she'd received from their dad. Levi had a big science project coming up and she didn't want him to be distracted from his work more than was absolutely necessary. His brilliant mind placed him years beyond his peers but his lack of confidence continued to leave him stuttering and hesitant when he had to speak aloud during an online class meeting. He fully understood the science principles behind his complex project but the idea of having to explain what he'd done, and why he'd chosen his topic, in front of his classmates terrified him. For this particular project, he would be scored 50% on the project itself and 50% on the oral presentation.

He was so terrified of public speaking, he contemplated taking a 50 and skipping the presentation altogether. The only way Abbey could talk him out of that was to remind him if he made an F on this assignment it would kill Mom. It would absolutely break her heart.

She didn't have Mom's patience with him. She listened while he practiced and tried to encourage him by offering helpful suggestions on his delivery but often her remarks made him feel worse than he already did. The waiting was also hard on him. His project had to be submitted several days before he had to give the accompanying oral report on what he'd done. For Levi, the anticipation of fear was greater than the fear itself. His science teacher needed time to examine every project and grade each of them. Abbey thought it was cruel to make little kids hurry up and turn in a project and then sit back and wait before they had to talk about it.

She decided to mark 'schoolteacher,' off her list of possible future jobs. She got too frustrated, much too quickly. Patience was a virtue she clearly lacked.

Her mom's phone rang. It was the same unknown caller as last night.

"Now, now Rose, don't hang up on me again. Let's let bygones be bygones. I'm just passing through and thought I'd like to check in on you, that's all. No need to get bent out of shape. Hello? Hello? Are you still there?"

Abbey answered, "I'm here."

"Whew! So, you're talking to me? That's good, That's real good. I don't mean to make no trouble. I just thought I'd stop in and say "hey," and what-not and then be on my way."

Abbey remained silent.

"So, what do you say? You still in that apartment over by the four corners? We sure had us some good times there, didn't we, babe?"

Who are you calling "babe," you old creep? Abbey's first instinct was to tell him the truth about where they lived but her desire to protect her family from her dad's intrusion was stronger than her need to stay in good standing with the heavenly powers that be. Lying was strictly forbidden and lying to your parents was strictly forbidden to the tenth power. She couldn't remember a time when she had broken so many Commandments simultaneously. There was the one about honoring your parents, the one about lying. Coveting a cell phone. Her mind knew these things but her tongue held sway. She did not want her dad knowing exactly where they lived. She could imagine how hurtful it would be if he made a habit of dropping in whenever the whim hit him. Levi would be in a state of constant emotional turmoil. She felt an overwhelming need to protect Levi and her mom from the walking heartache named Samuel Whit.

"We are. However, we're house sitting this week. At the house on Live Oak Drive. The people who lease the house got quarantined out of state. They asked us to look after their house. And their cat," she said. She didn't bother crossing her fingers when she lied. This was straight up gangster lying, no need pretending anything else. She'd ask for forgiveness later.

"Huh. Live Oak, you say? Where abouts on Live Oak would that be?"

Abbey couldn't believe he didn't remember the house that had ruined his and her mom's marriage. At least that's what she had always believed. "834 Live Oak Drive. It's a dead-end road. Second house on the right," she said.

"Well, OK then. What's a good time for you? Cause I can make it any time. You still working, right? You get off round about six, don't you?"

"As a matter of fact, I'm not working today," Abbey said. "Bank holiday." She knew there was no bank holiday but apparently her dad didn't keep up with such things. She gathered from her dad's remarks last night (about the time he stopped by her mom's bank), that he knew where Mom worked and apparently wasn't shy about busting up in there and embarrassing her in front of her boss and co-workers. She couldn't allow him to pull that stunt again, causing trouble for Mom. And she didn't want to risk him finding out about Mom being in the hospital.

"How 'bout that? Yesiree Bob! Guess today's your lucky day. I got myself a little business proposition to take care of, you know how that goes. Things are looking up for me these days, Rosie. Yes, sir, a sweet little business deal to take care of and then I can just drop on by. 834 Live Oak, you say? House sitting. Exactly how does that work anyway? Is there money to be made just by sittin' around somebody's house? Might be something I outta look into. You know me, always got an eye out for a new business adventure. Anyways, be seein' you soon."

Abbey turned to Levi and said, "As soon as you finish with your math work, come on in the kitchen and eat your lunch. And, don't forget your science project is due tomorrow morning. You'll need to get that out of the way too. I'm going to fry up some okra for you."

Levi was so happy about fried okra he jabbered on and on and didn't notice Abbey wasn't talking. Finally, Abbey said, "Levi, I got a phone call today. I don't want you to be upset. But the call was from Dad. I told him he could stop by here and see you."

Levi's face turned white, then red. He jumped up from the table and said, "Do I have time to take a bath? Do you think it'd be too much if I put on my good jeans? I want to make a good impression. He hasn't seen me since I was a baby." He kissed Abbey on the cheek and said, "What'd I tell you? I knew he'd come back! I knew it, Abbey!"

"Don't get your hopes up, Levi. He isn't moving back to town or anything. He's just coming by for a visit."

"I know. Hey, do you think he'll stay and eat supper with us? Of course, he will! Bet you he'll be surprised at what a good cook you turned out to be. I'm going to take a bath. When did he say he'd be here?"

"He didn't give me a specific time. He said he had some business to do and he'd stop by later." Abbey hated to admit to herself that she was as excited as Levi was. She wanted her dad to be proud of her and Levi. And she wanted him to love them. *I still hate him, but I can't spurn him if he doesn't care about me,* she rationalized.

She brushed her teeth and hair and put on a clean shirt and pants. With online school she hadn't been bothering to do much about her appearance, she usually wore the same sweatpants or pajama bottoms and tee shirt for a week before switching it out. She noticed the envelope in her top bureau drawer. Her savings for the cell phone. She hadn't bothered to think about that lately. *Bigger fish to fry,* she thought. Just like her great-great gran had thought so long ago. $420.00. A literal fortune. Funny, it didn't mean a thing to her any more. The girl who had been preoccupied, scratch that, *obsessed,* with a new phone no longer existed.

Without thinking of what she was doing, or why, she slipped the envelope into the pocket of her sweatpants.

When the doorbell rang, she forced herself to take her time instead of racing down the stairs. Levi was still in the bathroom getting himself decked out. *Guess that business deal didn't take as long as expected,* she thought. And then the truth of it occurred to her; there hadn't been a business deal. Maybe he felt bad about staying away for so long he was ashamed and felt he needed an excuse for visiting his children*: Couldn't spare the time to come by earlier, all this business I'm doing takes all my time.*

She opened the door to find a nice-looking older man standing on her front porch. He was dressed in faded jeans and combat boots. Sort of like a biker in movies. A big metal chain ran through his belt loops into his back pocket, maybe holding his keys or wallet? His faded black tee shirt advertised a band she had never heard of – *Fog Hat*? Maybe it wasn't a band, could be a brand of shirt for all she knew. Maybe a town he'd lived in.

He didn't look much like the few pictures she had of him. His dark hair was almost white. He wore it in a long braid down his back. He didn't match her mom, she thought. Mom was always well put together, kind of elegant, even without trying. This man, her dad, looked ill-kempt and tired. He had bags under his eyes and deep crow's feet. He smelled like motor oil or maybe it was engine exhaust, and cigarettes.

"Well, hello there, little lady." He strained to look around Abbey and into the house.

In the street in front of their house, a pretty young woman in a too tight jean skirt, smoking a cigarette, struggled to close the door on their car. Abbey didn't know much about cars but this one looked the worse for wear. It was some kind of low-slung job, with what looked to have been an outline of a giant bird of some kind, barely visible now, on the hood. The back doors were painted a dull, faded black. The rest of the car was light blue.

The passenger door screeched and refused to close completely. The woman finally gave up and left it ajar. She wiggled and jiggled up the sidewalk to join Abbey's dad on the front porch. The lady's build and coloring reminded Abbey of her mom. *Guess dad has a type.*

"I told you, you could wait in the car," her dad said to his companion.

"And, I told you, no I would not," she replied with a smile that belied the edge to her voice.

Good for you, Abbey thought. *Don't let him push you around.*

"Abbey! Is he here?" Levi ran down the stairs and came to an abrupt halt. "Oh, hi. You're here."

"And who's this fine young man?" Dad asked.

"This is your son, Levi. And I'm your daughter, Abbey. Mom's running errands."

Levi stumbled out onto the porch and hugged his father. "Hi, Dad. I knew you'd come and see us one day."

"Well, a-course I'd come. When I called her last night, your mom kinda suggested it'd be better if I didn't come over 'but Rosie,' says I, 'aren't they my kids too?' So, here I am. Running errands, you say? Funny she didn't mention that when I talked to her just now."

You are lying through your teeth, Abbey thought. *Maybe lying is an inherited trait. That would explain why it's been coming so easily to me lately.*

"Abbey? Boys-howdy, you have sure grown up into a fine young woman. What are you now, fourteen? Fifteen years old?" Dad said.

Abbey answered, "Yes, sir. Something like that."

"Humph, hum…" the woman pretend-coughed and said. "Aren't you going to introduce me, Sam?"

"Sure, sure. This is my, ah, my friend. Mandee."

She held out her hand to Abbey. She had rings on most of her fingers. The fourth finger of her left hand was bare. "Fiancée. Mandee. With two "ee's" Very nice to make your acquaintance."

"Nice to meet you, Miss Mandee," Abbey said. "And, this is Levi," she said, introducing her brother to Mandee.

Up close Mandee looked older than she did from afar. Like Abbey's dad, this woman had deep lines around her mouth and eyes. Without all the makeup, Abbey thought she'd be much prettier. *Why does he like you so much more than he likes our mom?*

"What do you say we take this party inside? How about it, Abbey? Invite your old man in?" Dad said.

"You can't smoke inside. Levi has asthma. And, you have to wear a mask. We have to be careful. Wait here please." Abbey pulled Levi inside after her and got masks for all of them.

Mandee blew smoke out of the left side of her mouth, tilting her chin upward as she did so. She crushed her cigarette out on the top step. Abbey gave masks to her and Sam and held the door open for them.

"This is some place you got here!" Mandee said. "You didn't tell me you owned a big house, Sam. You said you was just renting out a little apartment in town for your kids. You been holding out on me?"

"This isn't Dad's house. Or ours. We're house sitting," Abbey said. *Boy, once you start lying, it sure comes easier. Practice makes perfect.* Her dad had probably been practicing for years. Paying their rent in the old apartment? *Give me a break.*

Before Levi could contradict her about the house, she asked her dad and Mandee if either of them wanted a glass of sweet tea or maybe water. They both declined. She led them into the living room where her dad took a seat. Mandee asked if she could use the 'little girl's room.' Abbey directed her to the powder room, thankful they had toilet paper in there today.

Levi walked in tandem with their dad and squeezed in beside him on the recliner. "I'm doing a science project on the stable orbital resonance of dwarf stars," Levi blurted out. Abbey's heart went out to the poor little guy. He was so nervous.

"Is that so? Them words is about as big as you are, buddy. You must really love astrology," Dad said. "Well, sir. Yes indeedy. This is a mighty fine place. How much would you say its worth? In general? Me and Mandee's been thinking about buying us a little place like this. As an investment you know."

"I have no idea," Abbey answered.

Mandee joined them in the living room.

"I was just telling Abbey here, and little Eli..." Dad said.

"Levi," Abbey corrected him. "His name is Levi."

Dad turned to Mandee and said, "Yeah. Right. I was just sayin' to Abbey that you and me was thinking of buying up places like this as investments. Flipping, it's called. Buy low and sell high," he said. "People make a fortune doing that. Just need business savvy and there you go! Before you know it, you've made a bundle. Also don't hurt that your old man is what you might call "a jack of all trades." A little carpentry, a little engine repair, some body work here and there. I've done it all."

Mandee gave Dad the side eye. "Sure would be nice to have a house like this though," she said to no one in particular.

Dad's knees were jumping up and down. Abbey couldn't tell if he was anxious about something or if he was just a nervous kind of person who couldn't keep still.

"Well, this is a little awkward, you say your mom's out running errands? I was hoping to maybe talk to her about something. You don't know when she might be coming back?" Dad asked Abbey.

"Probably not for a while. You know how it is with Covid everywhere. You might have to go to lots of places just to get a few things. And the few businesses that are still open only allow a few people in at a time," Abbey said. "I'll be happy to give her a message for you though. Let me get a pad and pencil." She got up and walked into the dining room to get paper from her 'school desk.'

Her dad followed her to the dining room. "This is a little awkward," he said.

"Yes, sir. You just said that," Abbey said.

"The thing is, Abbey. I had me a string of bad luck. And, to be truthful with you, I was hoping maybe Rose would spot me a few dollars. Just a loan a-course. I am a man who pays his debts. I'm running low on gas and my spare tire's about flat. But, if she ain't home..."

Abbey took the envelope out of her pocket and handed it to her father. "Here, Dad. Take it."

He opened the envelope and fanned the money. He whistled, "Where'd you get this much loot? You didn't rob a bank, did you, hon?" He tried a weak laugh that fell short.

"No, Dad. I was saving my allowance for an emergency. I guess this is it."

"Well, I'll be. Things must really be going good for your mom if even her kid has this kind a money. I'll pay you back, Abbey girl, I promise. I can't tell you what this means to me. But, don't you worry, I will surely pay you back."

"Don't worry about it, Dad. I know you will."

You know he never will, Gran whispered.

It doesn't matter. He needs it more than I do, Abbey thought. *Besides, If I expect to get something back from him, it wouldn't be a gift. I don't want him coming around just because he thinks he owes me something. It's a gift. He helped give me life. I'll help him put gas in his car. We're even.*

Her dad patted her on the back. She went in and hugged him. "Take care of yourself, Dad."

"You bet. You too, Abbey." He pocketed the money and walked back into the living room. "Well, it's sure been nice but we need to hit the road. We're burning daylight here."

Mandee walked to the front door and handed her mask to Abbey.

"That's OK," Abbey said. "You can keep it."

When she opened the front door, Abbey was surprised to see her neighbors there. Mr. Lowe stood at the end of the sidewalk with a rake in his hand. Mrs. Patel was halfway up the front lawn with her cell phone out, taking pictures. Mr. and Mrs. Shaw had taken up posts to the far left and right of the yard.

"What's this? The welcome wagon?" her dad said. He took a step back inside the house as if the neighbors frightened him.

Abbey said, "No, sir. This is the neighbors. Our friends."

"We saw the strange car and came over to make sure Abbey and Levi were all right. Everything OK here, Abbey?" Mr. Hikara said from his position on the top step. He pulled a clean, white handkerchief from his back pocket and bent to retrieve Mandee's cigarette butt from the porch step.

"Yes, sir. Everything's fine," Abbey said. "Everything's just fine. Our dad was passing through town and stopped in for a visit." Her heart swelled with love for her friends and neighbors and she sent up a joyful thanks to God for leading her family here, to this little house in this little neighborhood.

Dad and Mandee side shuffled past Mr. Hikara who did not yield his space.

Dad said, "Nice to meet you folks." Then, to Abbey and Levi, he said, "Y'all take care. Sure was good to see you. And tell your mom hello for me and sorry I missed her."

Mandee started down the sidewalk then returned to speak to Abbey and Levi who were standing beside Mr. Hikara on the front porch. "You are a lovely young woman. Thank you for letting us come by. He may not show it, but it means a lot to your dad," she said to Abbey. "And you are the spitting image of your daddy," she told Levi. "You'll be a heartbreaker one day," she said.

Hopefully not the kind that breaks the hearts of his wife and children, Abbey thought.

After a few tries, her dad's car started with a loud backfire and then, with a puff of blue smoke, he was gone. The neighbors stood their ground until Dad's car was clean out of sight. Abbey waved to all of them and thanked them.

Levi said, "He didn't even know my name."

"Of course, he knows your name. You're his son, Levi. He just had some brain fog or something."

"He thinks you're fifteen," Levi said and giggled.

"Yeah, well. I'm big for my age. I get it from our mama's people. Are you going to be OK, Levi?"

Levi shrugged. "He isn't what I thought he'd be. Guess I better get my science project finished up." He slumped off back into the house.

Abbey's heart ached for him. And, if she was truthful, for herself as well. *Guess I don't hate him as much as I thought I did.*

The kitchen phone was ringing. It was Miss Yvonne. "Everything OK Abbey?"

"Yes ma'am," she answered and then started crying. "Our dad was just here, Miss Yvonne. He's been gone for so long and I thought we'd never see him again and now I wish we hadn't. He didn't want to see me and Levi. He wanted to borrow money."

"I'm so sorry, honey."

"How did you know he was here? How did all of you know? Everybody was here in the yard. The whole neighborhood," Abbey said.

"We've been watching out for you ever since they took your mom to the hospital," Yvonne told her. "We take turns walking around the property every night. Once at midnight, then again around 3:00 a.m. I guess you could call us your personal neighborhood watch."

"You knew? You all knew Mom's in the hospital? And, you didn't turn us in to the police? Or child services?"

"Well, no. We talked it over and decided with all the uncertainty around Covid, you and your brother were probably better off here in your own home. You obviously have a good head on your shoulders. And, since you're old enough to drive we thought we'd just keep an eye on you and be here for you when you needed us. You may not know this but when Mrs. Hikara was only thirteen years old, her mother died and she had to take care of her four siblings for several years until her father remarried," Yvonne said.

"No, I didn't know that. I guess there's always been little girls who've had to grow up fast," Abbey said.

"Your mom will be so proud of you. You're a good daughter, and sister," Yvonne said. "I hope my girls will grow up to be like you."

Abbey stammered. She wasn't used to getting praise. "You have no idea how that makes me feel," she said. And she thought, *but, if yall knew I was only twelve years old…*

We can just keep that to ourselves for the time being, Gran said.

By the time she and Yvonne finished their conversation, Levi had abandoned his science project and gone upstairs. She went up to his room to check on him but his door was closed. She put her ear to the door and heard him sobbing. She tried the knob but the door was locked. She tiptoed back downstairs. She wasn't so good at giving comfort.

She looked at the materials for his science project spread out all over the dining room table. She plugged in the hot glue gun and set about assembling his project. His notes, like everything he did, were meticulous. She'd have no problem getting the project assembled even if she didn't understand most of it. She'd have this knocked out in plenty of time to get supper warmed up.

Chapter 22: *Dispensation (noun),* Exemption from Usual Rules or Expectations

Since she still hadn't heard from Davey, Abbey decided to go to the trailer where he lived to see if his father had heard anything from him. She knew Mr. Loftin was physically abusive but she hoped he reserved his abuse for people in his family. *How sick is that? You only beat up the people you're supposed to love and protect.*

As usual, she couldn't stay mad at Davey. She worried he could be hurt or sick. She had no way of knowing if he made it to his uncle's in Raleigh or not. She knew she would be furious with him as soon as she found out he was OK. But, until then, she needed him to just freaking call her already.

A few days after their dad's visit, Abbey made a hearty meal of chicken and dumplings and loaded up a plastic container full to take to Davey's. She hoped Davey would be home but if not, maybe his dad would be less frightening if she bribed him with food. If he was even at home. There was no landline phone at Davey's house and she had no idea what Mr. Loftin's cell number was, so, she couldn't call ahead.

She knocked on the trailer's flimsy door, then stood back several feet, her mask firmly in place, to wait and see if anybody was home. Davey's father pulled the door open and glared out at Abbey and Levi. "What do you want?" he said to them.

He had a scraggly looking beard and dark circles under his eyes. His stomach protruded out from under the wife-beater undershirt he was wearing. His sweatpants hung low underneath his stomach. Even from a distance, Abbey could smell the miasma of this man or the inside of the filthy trailer, or most likely, a combination of both.

"Hi. Mr. Loftin? I'm Abbey and this is my brother, Levi. We're Davey's friends. We were wondering if maybe you'd heard from him? We were just kind of worried and hope he made it to his uncle's house OK. His Uncle Larry? Up in Raleigh."

Mr. Loftin took a swig from the can of beer in his hands, crumpled the can, threw it out into the yard, burped loudly, and said, "You say you're friends of his, huh? Well, you can tell him for me that I don't care where he went. And no need of him crawling back here, with his tail between his legs, begging me to take him in. He's gone and far as I'm concerned, he can stay gone."

Mr. Loftin turned his back on the children and headed inside.

"Wait!" Abbey said. "You haven't heard from him either? Do you have a number for your brother? Or, your brother's garage? Maybe we could call him and check on Davey."

"Who do you think you are and why do you think you can bust up in my home and question me about my son? It ain't none of your business. I suggest you git off my property."

"Yes, sir. We'll go. We didn't mean any harm. We're just worried about Davey. And, we brought you some chicken and dumplings. I made them for you once before. Remember? Davey said you loved them," Abbey said.

"So. That's where the cooked meals come from? And that commie face mask. I should-a knowed there was a girl involved. 'Course he gets that honest. I never could resist a purty face neither." He gave Abbey a long appraising look. "Yeah, you're purty enough. Or, you will be once you fill out some. You sort-a look like his mama. Guess that's what kinda gal he prefers."

Abbey was so embarrassed she couldn't speak.

Mr. Loftin continued, "You just take your highfaluting ways and your charity food with you and go back to where you belong. I don't need your food or your worry. Davey's made his bed. He can go lay in it. Just leave me be and…" He didn't finish that thought. He burst into tears and went back inside. He slammed the door so hard it didn't close shut, it bounced on the door frame and came back open.

Abbey walked up to the trailer and put the food down on the top step. She called into the house, "We're leaving now, Mr. Loftin. I'm sorry we upset you. I'm just going to leave the chicken and dumplings here in case you get hungry later on. I made a double batch and you know you can't freeze chicken and dumplings. They get watery. It isn't charity. I just thought maybe you'd help us out by eating some so I don't have to throw it away. It's sinful to waste food."

She and Levi were silent on the walk back home. Neither of them knew what to make of Mr. Loftin.

"I guess maybe our dad isn't the worst one, after all," Levi said. "Poor Davey."

When they got back home, they went their separate ways. Eli, to study his words and Abbey to settle in on Mom's bed and read Virginia's journal. Elsa, who decided she was the queen-mother of the domain, had chosen Mom's bed as her favorite napping spot. "You know you're not the queen of Mom's bed, don't you?" Abbey told the cat. "When she gets back home you're going to have to find a new favorite place to sleep." Elsa opened one eye, gave that idea all the consideration it deserved, yawned, and immediately went back to sleep.

Dear Journal. November 15, 1922. Big changes have come with my 14th year of life. Annie Mae has added three children to our family. Papa says the more the merrier. Three more and we'll give old Mr. Doubleday a run for his money and start ourselves a baseball team. I surely do hope six is all we get though. That's a gracious plenty if you ask me. Which nobody ever does.

Good news! Papa and I are out of the textile business. Papa landed a job with a construction crew building up this new town that's underway (Trinity Hold is the town that used to be a mill hill but now has almost a thousand souls calling it home). They are stringing electric wires to every home and business and all the new houses will have an indoor outhouse just like they do in big cities up north. I hear tell that Mr. Vanderbilt installed about fifty indoor bathrooms up in his mansion, The Biltmore, over in Asheville, but that could be just crazy talk.

Still, looks like indoor plumbing is the way of the future! Lots of people thinks that's just plain nasty to have a room full of slop jars inside your house but I like the idea of this new modern age with all its wonders. I am mighty curious to learn just how an indoor outhouse will work.

My mama's brother, who I'd never met before now, is a big-shot with the electric corporation. He had to come to town and give the mayor and city council the lowdown on electrifying this whole place. He says that electric is so cheap to make that if the town will donate the land down by the river for the construction of the power plant, and then pay to install all the wiring to the houses, pretty soon everybody can have electricity for free. It's the cheapest *form of energy known to man, and having light in your home 24-hours-per-day, if you want it, will revolutionize life in America, says Uncle Wes.*

Annie Mae had Uncle Wes over to supper and we were all nervous as cats, never having entertained a Man of importance before. Turned out we need not have been nervous. He was mighty jolly and brought candy treats for all of us children. He told me I looked just like his dear departed Sister and that brought a tear to his eye when he said it. I love him for saying so even though I know it can't be true. My mama was beautiful and I am just plain me.

Soon as I can get Uncle Wes to himself, I intend to ask him questions about my mama when she was a little girl. I want to soak up every bit of information he can give me so I can hold it all in my heart forever. I am so mad at myself for not asking mama more about her life. When I was little, I guess I thought our lives would keep going on the way they were forever. I didn't know how cruel life can be and whisk your dearest love away from you while you aren't looking.

This will be my last year of school because I've taken all the classes offered at our community school and can't go any higher unless I go off to college. There is a teacher's college in Belmont, near Charlotte that's run by The Sisters of Mercy of the Roman Catholic Church (which, unlike some other Baptists in town, I do not hold against them. They do the Lord's work all day every day, how can anybody fault that?), that I have my mind set on attending. They usually don't take women under seventeen years of age but if I can get three references from people of good standing in the community, who can attest to my maturity, scholarship, and good character, they will consider my application.

My Uncle Wes (who is a great Man and well known in these parts), and my school principal have said they'll write letters for me. To my surprise, mean old Sister Edith (who finally caught herself a live one and is now married to Mr. William Denton, the mayor of Trinity Hold), says her husband will gladly stand for me and my family's good reputation. Papa is head of the construction crew building their new mansion on Main Street so that probably worked in my favor.

Dear Journal. June 9, 1923. Tomorrow will be our last day of school and I am sad *about that. I still await news from the teacher's college about my admission but am beginning to worry that maybe they don't want a nobody like me to blemish their reputation.*

Cat is the most beautiful girl in town. Every day we pass by one of papa's construction sites (how could we not when this town's all construction all the time), and the young men who work on the crews all hoot and holler and profess their undying love for Cat as soon as they see her pass by. Unless, of course, papa is overlooking their foolishness. He is bigger than all of them and would take a strop to anybody disrespecting his daughters.

Cat throws her pretty head back and blows air kisses at them and says, "Dream on, boys." Which I tell her is fresh and ladies don't act in such a way. But she pays me no nevermind. I guess if I was a popular girl like Cat I'd maybe flirt with boys too. When papa wasn't looking.

Dear Journal. June 11, 1923. Praise God from whom all blessings flow! When I got home from school yesterday, Annie Mae was waiting for me out on the front porch. She was grinning like Lewis Carroll's Cheshire Cat. She told me to close my eyes and hold out my hands. When I did, she put a letter there. I opened my eyes and was filled with fear and trembling. The letter was from the teacher's college. All five of my brothers and sisters made a ring around me and hollered, "Open it! Open it!"

They accepted me! I am college bound! They don't think I'm a blemish after all. I have so many plans to make and so many things to do before September 3, which will be my first day of class. I can't believe it. I folded and unfolded, read and reread the letter until it's about worn out. As usual, money will be a problem but Annie Mae says try not to worry, the Lord works in mysterious ways.

Dear Journal. July 15, 1923. They say there is a scholarship fund set up for exceptional young ladies (papa asks, exactly who is 'they,' and darn their sorry hides?). According to a letter from the college, I qualify for that fund, pending my grades after the first term of school.

The other day Uncle Wes and papa had a big blow-out about that very issue: funding for my school. Uncle Wes said mama had left an endowment for each of her children and that money should go toward our education. Papa said this was the first he ever heard of that and accused Uncle Wes of offering him charity. I am surprised they didn't come to blows. Papa cannot abide the idea of anybody offering him charity. It's as bad as spitting in his eye.

Annie Mae and I listened in with our ears to the door but the issue wasn't resolved as far as we could tell. I want this so badly I can taste it but my fate is up to my papa and the scholarship fund. I pray for patience and faith that all will work out according to the will of the Lord. I wish I was a better Christian girl and could stop this worrying.

Chapter 23: *Succor:* Comfort in Times of Distress

A few days after their dad's surprise visit, Abbey and Levi got a call from Miss Robin. It was only four in the afternoon so Abbey was terrified. Their usual time to speak with Mom was seven-forty-five at night. This deviation raised Abbey's hackles. She ran out to the back yard to take the call. She couldn't risk Levi hearing any bad news about their mom. Her mind raced and her heart pounded in dread.

"Is this Abbey?" Miss Robin said.

"Yes, ma'am." Abbey's voice was so constricted she could barely whisper.

"Is your brother there with you?" Miss Robin asked.

"No ma'am. He's doing his schoolwork. And I don't want him to hear bad news from anybody but me. Did our mom take a turn for the worse?"

"Oh, no, Abbey. Quite the opposite. She has had a turn for the better and if she remains like this overnight, we'll be sending her home in the morning. Would you like to speak with her? I can call you back on facetime so you can see how much better she is."

Abbey hadn't realized that she'd been holding her breath all this time. She let it out, and practically squealed,

"Are you kidding? Of course, we want to talk to her! I'm getting Levi right now."

She raced back inside where Levi was just finishing up his oral report on his science project. She moved to stand behind him so his teacher and classmates could see her. "I'm sorry to interrupt your class, Ms. Johnson, but Levi needs to take a very important phone call. It's from our mom in the hospital. She's better and her doctors are sending her home in the morning!"

Ms. Johnson and all of Levi's classmates cheered. Ms. Johnson said, "Oh my goodness! That's the best news we've gotten in weeks! Go talk to your mom, Levi. And don't worry about class this afternoon. I know you have plans to make. We're so happy for you. Oh, Levi, tell your mom you made an A+ on your science project."

Usually obsessed with his grades, Levi didn't even care this time. The only thing in the whole wide world he cared about was seeing his mom and getting her back home.

Mom assured them she was weak but well on her way back to perfect health. She asked Abbey to arrange for a car to pick her up at the hospital in the morning. She promised to have the discharge nurse call to let them know exactly what time. Levi yammered on and on trying to stretch out the call but Abbey could only smile. And cry. Happy tears for the first time in months.

Abbey called Miss Yvonne to let her know the good news. Yvonne served as the unofficial call center for the neighborhood and Abbey wanted everybody to know their mom was finally coming home. Abbey feared her mom's reaction when she learned that Abbey had decided to shelter in place with Levi this entire time. She knew she'd lose her allowance for the foreseeable future and would be grounded, which, during Covid didn't mean much, but none of that mattered. Mom wasn't going to die! She was coming back to them.

Covid had killed so many people already. Abbey felt such sadness for all of the families left behind, but, for today, she felt overwhelming joy to have been spared. Her grandmother's old timey stereo and record collection were in the living room. Levi was partial to the Motown greats like the Temptations and Smokey Robinson. Abbey was astounded by the genius of Aretha Franklin and could listen to her all day long. She and Levi selected their old school favorites, cranked up the volume, and sang and danced like nobody's business.

They ate their supper in the living room. Abbey let Levi have seconds of chocolate ice cream. She let him sleep in his clothes and told him he didn't have to take a bath if he promised he'd bathe in the morning before they left to pick their mom up at the hospital. She tried to text Davey again but his phone was still out of commission.

She fell asleep on the couch, her great-great grandma's journal open on her chest.

Dear Journal. October 3, 1924. I have nearly completed my first year of teacher's college. I was granted a weekend pass to travel home to spend time with my papa who is doing poorly with a heart condition. I am happy to report his doctor says because papa has a strong constitution he should make a full recovery. For this and so much more I am truly thankful.

Cat and the other siblings gather round me and ask dozens of questions about what life is like "on the other side of the world," which is not where I study, it only seems that way to children who've lived in the same tiny village all their lives without benefit of travel. I've missed them all and don't mind the questions one bit.

I try to love all of them equally but cannot help but hold a special place in my heart for Cat and Richard for the three of us are Janey's children. When we are alone, I tell them stories of our mama because I can't bear the notion they might forget her.

I opened the front door last night to find a strange young man standing there. "Good evening, Miss Virginia," he said as if we knew each other. He doffed his hat, thrust a bouquet of flowers into my hands, and asked for permission to come in.

Cat, who was standing behind me, spoke right up, took the flowers and said, "Come right on in. I'll just put these in water for Virginia."

Cat gave me a sly look as she passed by me on her way to the kitchen. If I read her right, she was not at all surprised by this person's appearance at our door. Turns out, he is one of the young men who apprenticed with my papa on the construction crew. I remembered his twinkling eyes and huge smile when Cat and I used to pass by on our way home from school. Cat had teased me about him often, saying, "Somebody's got a secret admirer." I told her to stop being cruel to me, she knew all the boys were crazy for her, not for me, the big, old tongue-tied lump that I am.

Not being used to attention from any man, I stood stock still and remained speechless. Annie Mae took me by the arm, led me into the living room, and motioned for Mr. Winford to follow. She told us to please have a seat while she went to fetch my papa from his sick bed.

All the children squeezed in around, beside, and at the feet of Mr. Winford tossing questions out at him like he was a curiosity of some sort. When papa entered the living room Mr. Winford stood and shook his hand. "Glad to see you have regained your strength, sir," he said.

"I am pleased to inform you that I am of sound mind and body, young man so don't be getting any notions that you can pull the wool over my eyes. You say you have an interest in courting my oldest daughter, Virginia. Is that right?"

I wanted the floorboards to open up and swallow me whole. I turned red with blushing from my forehead all the way down to my toes. Oh, to be so humiliated in front of my entire family! Surely, he was on a mission to see Cat. Papa was bound to have known that. I truly wished somebody like him could be my beau but I also knew that hope was useless. I feared my secret thoughts of this handsome young man had been found out.

"Yes, sir," that's correct. As you know my prospects for permanent employment are good. You, yourself have recommended I be promoted from carpenter to master carpenter. As you also know, I have wanted permission to call on Virginia for some time now, as soon as you deemed it fitting to do so. Your wife ran into me a few days ago at the five and dime and informed me that Virginia would be home soon and I was welcome to come by."

I was stunned. Annie Mae looked at me and smiled. Mr. Winford, whose given name is Raymond, stood and smiled as well. Pretty soon the whole family was standing around smiling and I figured I may as well join the crowd so I started smiling too.

Cat, who considers herself the expert on matters of love, said, "Perhaps Mr. Winford and Virginia would care to sit out on the front porch and converse for a little while."

Annie Mae agreed and offered to bring glasses of lemonade out to us. Mr. Winford said, "Yes ma'am. I am agreeable to that, thank you much."

The young'uns all scurried to beat us outside but Cat and Annie Mae caught them and turned them back around. Papa made a big show of pulling on the sash and making sure the living room window was up all the way and then he pulled his chair over and sat right in front of the window to read the newspaper.

With an audience removed from us by a living room wall, Mr. Winford and I sat in the wicker chairs (situated directly by the big living room window), on our front porch and had ourselves a fine conversation.

Chapter 24: *Filial (adjective),* Relating to or Befitting a Person's Child

Abbey and Levi had spent fifty-nine days wishing and hoping and praying for the ordeal to end and their mother to come back home. Both children knew how extremely lucky and blessed they were to have been spared from becoming causalities of the virus. Every one of their neighbors had a relative or friend who had died of the virus. Both of Drew's grandparents had succumbed, leaving Abbey's friend distraught.

Americans, like people all around the world, were bewildered and in mourning. Covid-19 was a wildfire that consumed everything in its path regardless of age, race, or social status. It often felt as if the whole world was holding its breath, with a fist clenched in their chest, causing their whole body to cramp up, waiting for something tragic to happen. Instead of imagining good fortune waiting around the corner, far too many feared the specter of death was the thing hiding close by. Unfortunately, for too many, tragedy did indeed land on their doorstep.

Abbey wondered if she would ever get over the never-ending, ever-present fear and dread with which she had lived for so long. Would she ever stop holding her breath, waiting for the second shoe to drop and tragedy and misery to slide in, unannounced and unwelcome.

When she learned of the death of Drew's grandparents, Abbey decided to tell Drew the truth about her and Levi's situation. She wanted Drew to know that she truly empathized with her. She loved Drew and Drew's grandparents who had so often included Abbey in outings with Drew and her siblings. They felt badly for Abbey because she didn't have grandparents of her own and tried always to include her and make her feel loved and wanted. They were kind, generous, and loving people who did so much for others.

On the other hand, Davey's dad and her dad, neither of whom had ever done anything for anyone but themselves, were both spared from this plague. Was nothing in life ever fair?

Drew was astonished at what Abbey had accomplished. She wished she could have been close by and could have offered help to her friend. Abbey asked Drew please not to tell Mrs. Anderson about her mom just yet. She knew that tender hearted Mrs. Anderson would disregard her own health and rush right over to scoop up Levi and Abbey and take them back home with her. Abbey had everything under control and couldn't bear the thought of leaving Gran's house. Drew told Abbey she must be the smartest and bravest girl in America.

Abbey knew better. She hadn't been brave at all. She had acted rashly and made many mistakes. She had leaned heavily on Gran and Davey to help her function. And, truthfully, she had relied on Levi. He looked up to Abbey, trusted her completely, and did everything she asked him to do. He wasn't a brat like Drew's younger brother. Levi never complained about doing chores or following rules. Bathing regularly was the only thing she had to stay after him about. He was a good kid and partner.

She realized she also had Mom to thank for the success of the past few months. Her mom had set everything in motion by organizing their home and their lives. Gran was correct in saying Abbey was like her mom. She was indeed a student and ardent adherent of her mom's philosophy of child rearing and homemaking. Her mom's penchant for making lists to keep herself organized, of planning meals for the whole week instead of just day-by-day, and having clearly established rules and consequences (which she had always explained to her children as logically as possible, with reasons for why things were as they were), had become her own character traits without Abbey realizing it.

Abbey was comforted by the order and symmetry of their lives. They took their meals together, had family meetings to discuss and often debate things that affected all of them. Mom kept an art box full of paints and papers and canvases, ribbons, pipe cleaners, a virtual craft store, so any time anybody felt the need or got a school assignment that required them to express themselves, they knew where to go to pull out supplies. That may have been a weird thing to focus on, but, in school, they had to do projects of one kind or another all the time. Rose's children never dreaded having to do anything creative because creativity was just one part of who they all were.

Drew's family drove Abbey to distraction. They were all wonderful people and Abbey loved them but she could never live with any of them. There was no structure to their lives. They came and went without anybody knowing exactly where anybody else was. Laundry was rarely folded and put away, everybody just went to the laundry room and grabbed what they needed out of the clothes dryer or laundry basket. They all ate on their own schedules, standing up by the kitchen island, or quite often in front of the television or in their rooms.

One time, Drew and Abbey were supposed to team-up to make posters for the school's bake sale and also to make cookies and cupcakes. Drew's mom, Mrs. Anderson, invited Abbey to their house to complete their projects and stay for supper. Instead of having everything ready so the girls could get started as soon as they arrived home from school, Mrs. Anderson had to make three trips to the store to get the necessary supplies. The thought of making a list *before* she shopped never crossed her mind. Drew's mom's idea of an art box was the broken crayons and dried out markers in the big basket in the kids' playroom. And her notion of a stocked pantry was the warehouse at Walmart.

She completely forgot she was supposed to make dinner for the girls, so they wound up ordering a pizza (which was delicious but arrived so late Abbey had to take hers home to eat). Drew's mom was happy and fun to be around but Abbey would much rather have her stick-in-the-mud but attentive to details mother. Rose Whit would never make it as a stand-up comedienne but if you needed somebody to depend on, Abbey's mom was the woman for the job.

After the bake sale fiasco, whenever they had to do school projects, Drew usually came over to Abbey's to use the supplies there and to ask Mom for advice on how to make stuff. Mom could draw and paint and sculpt and sew and was full of ideas about how to create just about anything. She couldn't cook but nobody was perfect. Drew's house was big and beautiful but when she needed help, she came to Abbey's tiny, cramped apartment.

Mom insisted on good manners. She taught her children to say, 'Yes, sir', and 'Yes, ma'am.' She practiced what she preached as far as religion went. She truly loved people, something Abbey often struggled with. She offered food and drink to every person who came to their door. And she loved her family. No doubt about that.

Mom thought she had been blessed above all others because of her family. Nobody in their ancestry had ever held an important position in society or amassed any fortunes but their mom truly believed her family was tip-top and she wouldn't trade places with anybody else in the world. There had been a time when Mom's high estimation of their family had been an embarrassment to Abbey. That was no longer the case. She didn't know when she'd changed her mind about her family, but somewhere along the way a change of attitude had surely come.

Dear Journal. May 5, 1924. Next week I will graduate from Teacher's College and am hopeful to obtain a position at Trinity Hold's newest academic institution, which is a high school in the middle of town.

Of greater joy and importance, Raymond and I will marry on June 30. He is the kindest, most thoughtful person I have ever known. His bright smile, earnest personality, and genuine humility won over not only my own heart but my family's as well. I could never have fathomed how much love my heart could hold for any one person. Until now.

He has drawn up plans to build a house for us. He is very proud of his designs and pours over the plans daily, looking for improvements that can be made. He says he intends to build a sturdy home that will stay in our family for generations. I'm not sure about that, children have to be free to travel where they please after they grow up. Still, it's a nice thought.

He purchased an empty lot on Live Oak Drive for us and spends much time there walking and thinking. He is planning to put three bedrooms, a dining room, and not one, but two bathrooms in our house. Papa and Annie Mae both think this is extravagant and a waste but Raymond insists he is planning for the future and that one day families will need all these spaces.

If I am ever blessed enough to have children, I will remember the things my mama taught me and pass them along in the hopes of keeping a part of her alive:

1. Have faith in God. Always.
2. Set a good example for your children. What you do speaks so loudly they can't hear what you are saying.
3. Education is important.
4. Never punish a child in anger. Punishment should be used for instruction, not to cause pain.
5. Be consistent. Set rules and then stand by them. Children should know what is expected of them.
6. Respect others and yourself.
7. Especially for girl children: keep your hair and body clean and odor free. Never leave home in an unkempt manner. Being clean is more important than being pretty.
8. Do not raise your voice, especially not in the house. Ladies should speak softly.
9. Organize your home. A willy-nilly approach to housekeeping and child rearing leads to chaos.

10. *Teach your children the importance of family. No matter what your monetary status, no person is ever poor who has a family that loves them.*

Chapter 25: *Euphoric (adjective),* Very, Very Happy

Abbey and Levi were both up before the sun. Neither of them wanted to eat breakfast but Abbey insisted because this was probably going to be a long day and both of them needed their energy. And, they needed to keep their wits about them. Today, they would leave their sibling kingdom and venture out into the world of grown-ups.

They logged on to their school but couldn't focus on their work. Abbey sent messages to all of their teachers telling them that Mom was coming home from the hospital and they'd make up any missed work as soon as they could.

When the phone rang, both children jumped out of their skins. The discharge nurse told Abbey that Mom would be ready to leave around noon. She asked if there would be transportation there to pick her up to take her home. Abbey assured the nurse that she and Levi would both be there to get their mom.

She called a taxi and arranged for it to come to the house, pick up Levi and Abbey, go to the hospital and get Mom, then deliver all of them back home. The dispatcher assured them he could have a car there at eleven-thirty. He made sure Abbey knew that every rider must be masked.

The driver would also take their temperature before allowing anyone into the car. Anyone with a fever would be left behind.

When eleven-thirty finally rolled around, Abbey and Levi were waiting outside on the porch. The driver got out of the car and waited for the children at the curb. She took both of their temperatures and since they were both normal, she allowed them to enter her car. She had instructions from her dispatcher about their destination and asked about their mom. They carried on a lively conversation about the damage done by Covid-19, and how it had affected everyone, all the way to the hospital.

Mom was waiting, in a wheelchair, in the front lobby. Abbey and Levi ran inside to her. There were doctors and nurses lined up, clapping for their mom, joyous that her story had ended happily. Miss Robin was there too. She couldn't hug anybody because of her position in the Covid unit, she didn't want to take a chance on spreading germs, but she smiled and waved at Levi and Abbey and cried tears of joy with them.

Abbey thanked everyone for taking good care of her mom. She and Levi left flowers from their yard and handmade cards for the health care providers. She knew God would surely bless these heroic men and women who, in caring for their mom, had preserved their home and their family. No amount of money could ever repay them, her thanks would have to do for now.

They glided home on cloud nine. Neither child took their eyes off their mother. She was weak and tired but in good spirits. She asked about the house and school and Mrs. Jarvis but Abbey told her maybe it would be better if they waited until they were settled in at home before they discussed such weighty matters. Being with Mom was something they had hoped and prayed would happen for so long. Now that it was here, they wanted to savor the exquisite joy they all felt.

They turned off the main road and onto their street where they saw the whole neighborhood lined up with signs and banners welcoming Mom home! Their driver honked her horn and rolled down all the windows in the car so Abbey and Levi could stick their heads out and cheer and wave at their friends. It was like a parade and Abbey and Levi and Mom were the only people on the float.

Abbey and Levi stood on either side of their mother, helping her get out of the car and then supporting her when she made her way ever so slowly up the sidewalk. Mom had lost so much weight she was practically swimming in her clothes. She was wearing the same outfit she had worn on her last day of work. The day the ambulance had come to their home and taken her to the hospital.

There were casseroles and desserts packed in dry ice inside coolers on the porch. Everyone had sent their specialties. Abbey wouldn't have to cook for at least a week. Maybe two. After getting Mom inside, Abbey went out to thank everyone and retrieve the food. She took the coolers inside with her so she could make a note of what came from whom. She would transfer all the food into her own containers so she could wash and return the neighbors' containers and coolers later. With thank you notes, of course.

Mom was plenty tired. She hadn't done so much moving around in weeks. The children helped her upstairs. Levi didn't want to leave her side but Abbey made him wait in the hall while she helped Mom out of her work clothes and into a soft nightgown. She took Mom's dirty clothes down to the laundry and allowed Levi to go in and sit on Mom's bed if he promised not to jump around.

Levi introduced their newest family member to his mom. Elsa, as usual, was sleeping on Mom's bed, her favorite spot. Mom was thrilled to have a cat in the house. She thought Elsa was absolutely beautiful. She said that pets help make every house a home. They weren't allowed to have pets of any kind in their old apartment, which made all of them sad. The addition of Elsa to the Whit household was a welcome change to the status quo.

Abbey logged in to find what class work she needed to do and found she only had one assignment for her literature class. She finished that quickly and went back up to check in on her mom. Mom was asleep with her arm around Levi who had also fallen asleep. She decided to crawl in beside them even though she wasn't sleepy. As soon as her head hit the pillow she fell sound asleep. Elsa begrudgingly scooted down to the foot of the bed and continued her nap, draped across Abbey's feet.

An hour later, Mom shook her and said, "Hey sleepy head. What's for supper?"

Abbey opened her eyes and burst into the happiest of happy tears. "Oh, Mom. You have no idea how happy I am to have you home! I love you so much, I wish I had Levi's vocabulary so I could tell you. I'm sorry for being such a pain in the behind and bugging you about a cell phone and talking back to you. I won't ever do that again. I promise."

Mom hugged her and said, "Thank God for keeping all of us safe. I'm the most blessed woman who ever lived. But, don't make promises you can't keep. We'll get back to arguing again any day now."

"But not today," Abbey said.

"No, not today," Mom answered.

Levi yawned and stretched and said, "Hey, Abbey. Is it supper time yet? I'm hungry. Did we eat yet today?"

"Not since breakfast and that was a long time ago. We can get the TV trays and bring food up here so we can eat with Mom. If that's ok with you, Mom. Do you feel like having us up here with you or should we leave you alone so you can rest?"

"I can rest anytime. I don't want to let the two of you out of my sight! I have missed you so badly, I'll probably make you sleep in here with me for a year!"

"Levi kicks, so that's a bad idea," Abbey said.

"Abbey snores," Levi countered. He laid back down beside his mom.

"Whatever. Hey! You're not lying back down. Get up and help me get everything ready. I'm not lugging all the food and trays up by myself. I'm not your maid," Abbey said.

"Ah, the sweet sounds of home," Mom said. Then, she swatted Levi on the butt and told him, "Scoot! Go help your sister."

"Yes, ma'am. I'm going." And he did. Elsa, hoping to score a cat treat, meowed loudly, thumped down off the bed, and followed her servants down to the kitchen.

They ate the most delicious vegetarian lasagna from Mrs. Lowe, followed by carrot cake with cream cheese icing from Yvonne. It tasted doubly delicious to Abbey because she didn't have to cook it. Eating somebody else's food reminded her of the good old days when they could occasionally go out to eat, before Covid shut all the restaurants down.

Levi helped Abbey take everything back to the kitchen and clean up what little bit there was to do tonight. Abbey told Levi to go on and take his bath while she finished transferring all of the neighbors' dishes into storage containers and placing them in the freezer. It was getting tight in there, she wouldn't have to shop online for a main course meal for a month. She loaded the dishwasher, wiped down all the counters, locked up the house, turned out the lights and headed up to check on Mom.

Levi was worn out from all of the excitement. He slept soundly on the sleeping bag he had dragged into his mother's room, his dictionary open where he dropped it beside him. Abbey asked Mom if she wanted her to wake him and send him to bed in his own room but Mom said, "No, let him stay." She told Abbey to get ready for bed herself. She was so tired she didn't think she could stay awake any longer.

Abbey bathed and put on her pajamas then went in to tell her mom and Levi goodnight. Both of them were sound asleep. Abbey tucked the covers in around both of them and kissed them goodnight. She hesitated for a moment before leaving her mother's room. She was filled with such love and thankfulness, she hoped she would always remember how close they came to losing each other and how important it was to be appreciative of each other. She knew they would continue to have fusses and misunderstandings, but she prayed she could always retain this little nugget of pure joy.

She scooped Elsa up into her arms, took her out of Mom's room, and closed the door. She didn't want Elsa biting Mom's toes and knocking everything off the dresser and nightstand at six a.m. to announce it was time for everybody to wake up to pet her, feed her, and just generally admire her beauty, as was her habit.

Back in her own room, Abbey opened Virginia's journal to a random page and began reading. She had never been one to read any book from front to back, she often read the last page first (which bugged her mom), and skipped around to pick up bits and pieces of narrative before settling in to read the whole thing from page one straight through to the end. No matter where she read in the journal, Virginia's stories touched her heart. She knew she would read the entire journal several times before putting it away for good.

Dear Journal, April 7, 1923. In literature class today we read 'My Heart Leaps Up,' by William Wordsworth. I am haunted by this poem. My mother and I consumed Emily Dickenson's entire output and hashed and rehashed what each word meant in all its variations. I never thought another poet would move me as she had. I still hold Dickenson dear because she reminds me so vividly of mama. But, Wordsworth! Ah, Wordsworth!

Mama and I never had a chance to read Wordsworth, we didn't have a volume of his poetry. Oh, but how I wish we had! I discovered 'Surprised by Joy' only last month and have pondered it in my heart constantly since that time. Like Wordsworth, I remember the first time after mama's death when I was surprised to feel a great happiness which I wanted to immediately share with her, only to instantly realize that she was gone. I could never share anything with her again. How could I have forgotten that, even for one split second?

Only a few weeks after our mother died, our papa was away from home. I, a young girl of eleven, was left in charge of my five-year-old sister and our eighteen-month-old baby brother. It was a bleak time. The cold, dark, dead of winter reflected the desperate loneliness and sadness within our hearts and our home. Mama was the embodiment of love and sunshine and when she left us, she took all of the warmth and light out of our family.

After quite a struggle I was finally able to get our brother to lie down for a mid-morning nap. I admit to needing a respite from him as much as he needed to rest after a full morning of exploring and crying and demanding that attention be paid. With a thankful heart, I managed to quiet him by rocking him in mama's old chair, humming the lullaby she always sang to us when we were babies.

He didn't stir when I laid him down in the center of mama and papa's bed, surrounded by pillows to keep him from falling off. I covered him in mama's nightgown so he would be comforted by the smell of her that lingered on that garment.

I shushed Cat and told her to tip toe so as not to waken our sleeping mischief maker. The sun was trying to shed its weak rays and burst through the gloom of the skies outside our house. That was a tall order even in the warm months because we lived in the middle of a pine thicket and sunlight was, even in summer, filtered through the woods in which our home stood.

We were thrilled by even the hint of warmth and I allowed Cat to remove her shoes and leggings. I set her down on the stump papa used to split wood for the stove on, and told her we could play her favorite game. She squealed and clapped her hands, free to make noise now.

My favorite game was "Jump Plank." I was bigger than most of our friends so when I jumped on my end of the plank, I could send my friends soaring up into the sky. Or, so it felt like to us. I hoped Cat would pick 'Jump Plank,' even though she was so little I wouldn't be able to jump hard with her on the other end of the plank for fear of causing her injury.

Cat's favorite game was "Tend Like." It was a favorite with most of the girls in our school. Though we didn't know it at the time, we all lived in poverty. Because all of the families we knew were in the same straights as we were, we simply thought not having adequate food or clothing and little to no toys, was the way of all life on the planet, with the exception of people in story books, *fairy tales, and Hollywood. "Tend Like," was the perfect escape for us.*

"Tend Like," is a game of "pretend." When I was little, I didn't know we were mispronouncing the word "pretend', " shortening it to "tend'." That was just how we spoke. Some considered speaking clearly and correctly a sign that someone was putting on airs. Sister Edith always spoke correctly. Even more so than our schoolteacher. I still don't know anything about Edith's level of education (had she gone to a fancy school like our mama had?). She obviously wanted the community to acknowledge her superior intellect. Which we did not.

Cat began, "Tend like... I'm a beautiful princess. What kind of dress would I wear?"

I told Cat she wore the softest, most luxurious velvet gown in the kingdom. Pink was her favorite color, so I told her it was pink. She loved ribbons so I added ribbons of every color and sparkling diamonds and emeralds and pearls on her gown and in her hair.

I picked the few wildflowers that hadn't yet succumbed to winter's devastation and wove them into a crown which I placed on Cat's head. I stripped the bark off a hickory stick and told her that was her royal scepter. She waved her scepter around, pointing to the chickens pecking in the yard and telling them they were the finest white horses in the land. She waved her scepter at Azalee, our milk cow, and told the cow she was the wicked old, recently dethroned queen. "Be gone from here, you wicked, wicked cow-queen!" Cat demanded.

Papa's hound, Brownie, sensing something happening in the front yard, came bounding out of the woods and tried to jump up and sit in Cat's lap and lick her in the face. "Oh, my! Sir Brown of Castle Canine, you mustn't jump upon your lady love. You will soil her velvet gown," I said.

At that precise moment, the sun which had struggled all morning, found renewed strength and burst through the clouds and the trees and the mid-winter's gloom to shine like a beacon on Cat's head. Her precious blonde curls became a halo framing her lovely face. She clapped her hands and laughed and for a moment I wanted to run inside and fetch mama so she could celebrate Cat's beauty and our momentary reprieve from the perpetual sorrow that engulfed us.

As suddenly as that thought crossed my mind, it was replaced by the overwhelming sadness of knowing mama would never celebrate anything with any of us, ever again. Equally strong was my guilt at having forgotten for even a second that our mama was gone. Dead and buried just a few feet away in the side yard, between her yellow rose bushes. I was 'surprised by joy'. Just like Wordsworth had been.

In "My Heart Leaps Up," Wordsworth muses that "the child is the father of the man." I cannot stop wondering if who I am now is intricately tied to the child I was then. Will I forever be the impoverished, motherless girl, weighed down by responsibilities thrust upon me much too soon? Will I carry this burden, like a clenched fist inside my soul, along with me forever? Is it such a bad thing if I do?

Chapter 26: *Denouement (noun),* The Final Part of a Narrative When All Is Explained or Cleared up; the Unraveling

Abbey and Levi were a little rusty at logging on and getting back to their regular schoolwork but it didn't take them long to pick up where they had left off two days ago. Now that Mom was back home, everything they did was an occasion to celebrate their reunited family. Eventually the everyday would become tedious again, but for the time being, life was to be savored.

After helping her mother bathe and wash and dry her hair, Abbey brought Virginia's journal into Mom's room and asked if they could talk about it. Mom agreed but said, "First, we need to talk about Mrs. Jarvis and you and Levi and the time I spent in the hospital."

Abbey knew this time would come but she still dreaded broaching the subject. She took a deep breath and plunged in. "To be perfectly honest, Mom, when I mentioned Mrs. Jarvis to you that night on the phone, I was sort of lying. More like, lying by omission. I didn't exactly tell you a lie but I didn't exactly tell you the truth either."

"So, there is a large gray area between the truth and a lie? Is that what you're telling me?"

"No, ma'am. I don't think so. I think the truth is the truth and a lie is a lie. The truth is, I lied to you about Mrs. Jarvis. And some other stuff too. Mrs. Jarvis didn't come over and stay with us and we didn't go over to her apartment and stay with her either." Abbey was so nervous her insides were shaking. She wiped her sweaty palms off on her pajama bottoms and continued. "But, before you get mad at me and ground me till I'm twenty-one, I'd liked to explain why I lied."

"Please do," Mom said.

Abbey explained her great fear of being separated from Levi. Of being placed in foster care or in an overcrowded, dirty group home somewhere, maybe even in another city while Mom was hospitalized. She told her mother how she agonized over the harm such a move would cause Levi, due to his young age, and to herself as well. She had held a family meeting and together she and Levi decided they couldn't bear to be taken out of their home. They rationalized that if Abbey was capable of babysitting all day during the summer while Mom was at work, the added extra hours between bedtime and waking shouldn't require additional supervision.

She added her fear of being around strangers during Covid was also a factor in her decision to remain alone, at Gran's. If Mom had been so careful to always wear a mask and practice safe distancing from others, and she still became ill, just how safe could a strange home or worse yet, a facility housing dozens of unfortunate children, be for Abbey and Levi? Levi's asthma made him especially vulnerable to the disease that attacked respiratory systems with a vengeance. In the end, Abbey accepted responsibility for the decision to remain at Gran's with no adult supervision. Looking back, she still felt it had been the right choice.

"I agree," Mom said.

"Really? You do?" Abbey was so relieved!

"Yes, Abbey, I believe staying here was the right choice. There was no perfect solution for us but I think you made a wise decision. The fact that we have such wonderful neighbors who stood ready to help out, has to be taken into consideration as well. I'm not so sure I would have wanted you alone in our old apartment complex with only Mrs. Jarvis to depend on. Truth be told, she needed you and Levi more than you needed her. And with her age and failing health, it's probably a good thing you weren't around her."

"That's what I said! Wait, what? You knew about the neighbors looking out for us?" Abbey said. "How? I only found out a few days ago."

"My Covid nurse, Robin, is Yvonne Dale's sister. After I regained my faculties enough to know what was going on, she shared stories from her sister about my magnificent children. She was especially impressed by the maturity, kindness, and abilities of my daughter. As am I. You are a remarkable child, Abbey. I don't know why God blessed me with such extraordinary children but *he* surely did."

"Wait a minute, you knew we stayed here alone. But you still asked me about Mrs. Jarvis?"

"I wanted to give you the opportunity to tell the truth, Abbey. Confession is good for the soul. I'm sorry you had to grow up so fast. I'm sorry about all of this. What a horrible year it's been for us. For the world."

"Yeah. It pretty much sucked. I know you hate that word but it's accurate. I bet even Levi couldn't come up with a better adjective."

"Verb. It's a verb, not an adjective. Past tense of 'suck,' is 'sucked'," Mom corrected her.

"You word people kill me! Why am I the only person in this family who isn't in love with words?"

Levi came in and said, "Mom and I are just lucky, I guess. Sorry, Abbey. But you got the good-cook-genes. That's more practical anyway. Mom and I can't even make cereal. Hey, Abbey, did you tell Mom about Gran yet?"

"Haven't gotten around to that part yet. Ah, Mom, this might sound weird or far out and freaky, but sometimes Gran talks to me. I can hear her voice inside my head."

"Yes, she has a tendency to do that," Mom said. "On occasion. Even in the hospital I often felt like she was near me. When I got scared or so tired, I could hear her urging me on, telling me to be strong for my children. Just like she always did when you guys were little. She constantly reminded me of how important every minute with you is. To never waste an opportunity to show you how much you were loved. Sometimes I still think I can hear her voice clearly in my mind. It's a great comfort to me. I hope it was for you as well."

"It was. I mean, it has been for a while now. It still is," Abbey said.

"Yeah, Abbey thinks we live in a haunted house and Gran walks around here and talks to her. I try to see Gran but I can't see her like Abbey can. Tell Mom about the time you saw Gran standing at the top of the stairs. It was really spooky," Levi said.

"No, it was not spooky, Levi. And I'm not positive, I actually saw her. Maybe it was a trick of the lights. You know they flicker on and off sometimes." Abbey was glad she had never told Levi about her encounter with Gran and the "Mom Cave." She needed to keep that secret in her heart. Maybe it had been real. Maybe it had been a dream. Either way, the thought of the energy of all our mothers' love being a tangible thing was comforting. She liked the idea of being connected to God and the universe *he* had created. Who was she to say whether or not such a place existed? With God, all things are possible. Even the freaky, far-out improbable places, people, and things.

"Have you been reading Virginia's journal?" Mom asked.

"Yes, ma'am. And I love it! Sometimes it's so sad it makes me cry but sometimes there are happy stories in there too. And I love Virginia! I wish I could have known her. Sometimes she is so funny. I don't know if she means to be or not, but sometimes she cracks me up. Did you know Virginia and her family lived through the Spanish

Flu pandemic that's almost exactly like the Covid pandemic?"

"I'd forgotten about that. But, yes, it's quite a coincidence. If you believe in coincidence. I prefer to believe God just sends us messages we need to hear when we need to hear them. I remember when I was young reading *Great Grandma Virginia's* journal. She became so real to me I thought I could see her and hear her voice. Maybe that's what happened to you, Abbey. Being lonely and worried about me and reading about the trouble's life threw at your great-great grandmother made you sensitive to her and to my mother. You've always had such a vivid imagination, I can see why you would believe you could actually see and hear one of your grandparents."

"So, you think I imagined it? Gran really didn't talk to me and show me, well, magical places?"

"That's not what I'm saying at all. My mother was the most stubborn, strong-willed person I've ever known. And she had the faith that could move mountains. If anybody in history ever had the power to travel back and forth through different plains of existence, I'd place my money on your gran. That woman!" Mom shook her head, smiling at the thought of her mother.

"Did I ever tell you the story of when I was about ten years old and went out too far in the ocean and got scared because my feet didn't touch the sand? Just as I started to panic I felt myself being lifted up by two strong arms. Mama, who weighed about a hundred pounds soaking wet and who couldn't swim and was deathly afraid of the water, had come on out to rescue me. The undertow was strong that day and every wave knocked both of us down and pulled us further out into the sea. I don't know how she did it, but she got both of us back to shore."

"Maybe it was really you who got the two of you back. I know you've always been a good swimmer," Abbey said.

"No, Abbey. I was exhausted and scared to death. All I could do was cling to my mama. I buried my head in her chest and she carried me like I was a baby in a sling. I remember thinking that if I was going to die, at least I'd die with my mama."

"Later that night, I asked her how she thought she could possibly save me when she couldn't swim. She said, 'The Lord would have given me the ability to walk on the water if that's what it took to get you back to shore'. And maybe that's what she did. I don't know. I know she believed it with all her heart and didn't hesitate to act on that faith."

"I sure wish I knew her, Mom. She'd love me, wouldn't she? And she'd rescue me if I was ever to need it, wouldn't she?" Levi asked.

"I told you, Gran does know you, Levi. And she loves you and she watches out for you," Abbey said.

Mom said, "Abbey's right. I think Gran knows you and loves you. Her love for all of us is strong enough to make miracles happen."

Abbey said, "You're saying you think it could have really happened? I could have actually seen Gran and heard her speak and maybe even walked around the backyard with her?"

"'There are more things in heaven and earth, Horatio, than are dreamt of in your philosophy'. Sorry, you haven't read *Hamlet* yet, have you? There's so much more to the universe and to our existence than any of us can imagine. Our brains just aren't powerful enough. Besides, if something is real to you, is it not real? If Romeo and Juliet *thought* they were in love, were they *not* in love because some adult somewhere said they were too young to understand what love is?" Rose tried to speak to her children as if they were intelligent people, not dumb kids. Abbey had forgotten about that.

"Yeah! And speaking of Romeo and Juliet, did Abbey tell you about Davey? How he was always over here because he's in love with Abbey but then his dad beat him up and he had to hitch a ride way off somewhere and go live with somebody else?" Levi was on a roll.

"Interesting," Mom said. "Abbey, do tell."

So, Abbey told her mom all about Davey. Mostly all. She waited until Levi went to bed to confess her true feelings. She didn't want Levi to make a joke of the way she felt. She'd never felt that way about anybody. Drew had already been in love at least four times but this was all new for Abbey. It wasn't a feeling she cared to expose to public ridicule.

Mom shared with Abbey her own story about the first boy she ever loved. His name was Max and she met him in junior high. Max was all she could think about for months. Actually, for years. She wrote his name on all of her notebooks. She dreamed of a day when Max would turn and look at her and finally see her for who she was. Sadly, that day never came. Max was head-over-heels in love with Heather, a beautiful real-life Barbie doll kind of girl. Mom couldn't compete with that. The last she heard of Max and Heather, they had sailed off into the sunset together, both going to college in Chapel Hill.

"Do you ever still think about him?" Abbey asked.

"Not in years. But, you know, funny thing, I dreamed about him last night. We were at a football game at our old high school, and he was sitting by himself. I was so happy to see him. I started to walk over to him but a huge ocean wave crashed over the bleachers and washed the stadium away. Poor Max."

Abbey started laughing. "Yeah, poor Max. That's what you get for messing with a woman who has the ancestors watching out for her."

Mom joined in the laughter. It was so good to be home. The road to recovery would be long. There would be false starts and set backs, but, in the end, their family would face all obstacles together and they would prevail. Just like they always had.

A Deeper Dive

1. Fictional characters must be believable and consistent. Compare the character of Abbey from the beginning of the book to the end of the book. In your opinion, is her progression believable and consistent?

2. Compare and contrast Davey's father with Abbey and Levi's father.

3. What are some parallels between Abbey and her great-great grandmother Virginia? What are some differences?

4. In the beginning of the novel, Abbey has a singular motivation. As the novel progresses, her motivation changes. Discuss Abbey's motivations and why and how they change.

5. Did Gran actually appear to Abbey and speak to her? Discuss why you believe as you do.

6. What is the significance of each chapter being a vocabulary word?

7. If you were in Abbey's position, would you have made the same decision about staying at Gran's and raising Levi by yourself? Why or why not?

8. What do you think happens to Davey in the future? What are some reasons why he doesn't contact Abbey after he leaves home?

9. Most humans are complex characters. Why do you think Davey's father burst into tears?

10. Why do you think Virginia hated the little brown envelopes containing her weekly pay from the mill?

11. Verisimilitude means "having the appearance or feeling of being true to life." Choose an episode from this book that enforces the verisimilitude of the story for you.

12. Virginia wonders if she will carry the sorrow of being the girl who lost her mother with her always. Do you believe she will?

13. Because literature is basically about what it means to be human, sometimes the story's setting is of little importance. How and why is the setting (time and location), in this story important?

14. Do you believe Virginia was successful in imparting the wisdom of her mother to her progeny?

15. What are some habits or philosophies that are shared by members of your own family?

16. Poetry plays an important part in Virginia's story. Describe a time when a poem or song, touched your heart and expressed an emotion(s) you were feeling at the time.

17. Choose one of the following themes found in this story and use textural examples to show how the author illustrates that theme:

   a. Faith
   b. Family
   c. Siblings
   d. Friendship
   e. Morality
   f. Responsibility